EVERYMAN'S RULES

f
o
r

SCIENTIFIC LIVING

A Novel

CARRIE TIFFANY

SCRIBNER

New York   London   Toronto   Sydney

SCRIBNER
1230 Avenue of the Americas
New York, NY 10020

First Scribner edition 2006

Originally published in Australia in 2005 by Pan Macmillan Australia Pty Ltd.

For information about special discounts for bulk purchases,
please contact Simon & Schuster Special Sales:
1-800-456-6798 or business@simonandschuster.com

DESIGNED BY LAUREN SIMONETTI
Text set in Goudy Old Style

Manufactured in the United States of America

1   3   5   7   9   10   8   6   4   2

Library of Congress Cataloging-in-Publication Data
Tiffany, Carrie, [date]
Everyman's rules for scientific living : a novel / Carrie Tiffany.—1st Scribner ed.
p. cm.
I. Title.
PR9619.4.T545E95 2006
813'.6—dc22   2005044529

ISBN-13: 978-0-7432-8637-4
ISBN-10: 0-7432-8637-5

For TPS, TES, & GRT

CONTENTS

EVERYMAN'S RULES

for

SCIENTIFIC LIVING

1

THE BETTER-FARMING TRAIN BRINGS SCIENCE TO THE MAN-ON-THE-LAND

1934

There are days of slow chugging through the wheat. I look out the window at the engine as it rounds a bend. Living on a train is like living inside the body of a snake. We are always leaning into the curves, always looking forwards, or backwards, never around. Here we are arriving at some tiny siding, just a few neat-edged buildings and their sharp shadows. Here we are again, a few days later, pulling away, all of us craning out the windows, gazing down the long canyon of railway line.

Sometimes a grateful farmer, or his son, will run a length beside us, waving his hat and grinning and calling out, "Three cheers for the Better-Farming Train," as if we are going to war. In those few days at Balliang East or Spargo Creek or Bendigo we make a place like somewhere else. Somewhere new.

The children say, "Look, a circus, look at the tent, look at the animals."

Time moves differently around us. Our lecturettes, illustrated

1

with lantern slides, show the same farmer, time after time, about his chores. There he is, before breakfast, caring for his dairy herd in the wet hills of Mirboo North. A row of Eaglehawk graziers watches him closely and they bray with disbelief at the lush green of the pasture, although the slide is in black and white.

"Again," the men say. "We want to see it again."

We bring to each town new sizes and shapes and colors. Beasts broader than they are high; cows with giant dangling udders whose teats brush the ground like the fingers of a glove; fleece-laden sheep like walking muffs; wheat grown so high by colorless chemicals it reaches the waist of the tallest man. Our fruits and vegetables on display are large and smooth and perfectly formed. They gleam, inviting touch, and give off a sweet, waxy aroma.

The women's car is at the end. Fourteen cars of stock and science and produce and then us, a shiny afterthought: infant welfare, cookery, and home sciences. My colleagues—Sister Crock, head of "women's subjects," and Mary Maloney, lecturer in cooking—complain about our position. Or rather Sister Crock complains. She says it is a question of cinders. When the train turns a corner cinders blow back through our windows into our kitchen, onto my dressmaking dummies, dressed and swaying.

Mary Maloney and I smirk. Because she raises this complaint in the Mallee, where we chug along for days, as if drugged, pushing through the endless wheat. There are no corners, no hills, no ridges, no edges to anything. At the Minyip siding I notice that the men of the wheat districts are straight-backed and stiff-necked. Many seem dazed at the sight of us. They are men with no experience of corners.

The cinders are not the real reason Sister Crock complains.

2

Being at the end means that when we have finished our lectures at one town and packed up to travel to the next, we must walk through all the agricultural cars to the sitting car up front. Sister Crock says when a lady travels she must be seated. She says, "Oh lordy, lordy," clapping a white handkerchief to her nose in the pig car.

Each car is a tunnel of smell. The air moves in through open slats, across the beasts, across us walking up the aisles, and then mixes together behind the train into a heady, steamy cloud. Only the animals grazing in the paddocks as we pass can unmingle the odors and reply in loud yearning to a juicy cow or the sharp piss of a colt in his prime.

We jam Sister Crock between us. Mary is on shit alert. She says, "Jump now, Sister," as a huge Border Leicester ram aims a clod of pellets in front of us. They fall like marbles and we hop about on our toes to avoid them. Sister Crock shakes her head. We have an effect on the animals. It's not just the shit; they moo and bah and grunt and bellow at us, even after we've gone, but perhaps a little more forlornly.

"We're starting them up," Mary says, smiling at me. And we are. The cacophony of each car is dulled a little by the chorus of the one before.

The dairy car is next. Mary and I like to linger in dairy implements. She is a real farm girl, not like me. Sister Crock had her on recommendation—a nimble girl and a handy cook. Mary's father was reluctant to let her go and now he sends messages for her; they follow us down the stalls from dairy to dairy, on a milk cart, on a truck, refreshed at a tiny hotel and then spoken by an awkward man hoisting himself into our women's car. "The

Maloney girl," he'll say. "I have a message for the Maloney girl."
Mary dusts her hands or smooths down her apron as the man,
always a similar-looking sort of man, blushes. "Your father, your
father says keep well . . . and he loves you."

Sometimes they leave off the last bit, the love refrain. And
we know they had meant to say it, right up until they swung
into the car and saw us, three women on a train full of animals,
playing house.

Mary drinks in the dairy implements. She explains to me
what she knows, the indoor stuff of cream separators and churns
and pats and butter makers and thermometers and hygienic
wraps. Mary's future is in cows. She is secretly engaged to
George, the son of a neighboring dairy farmer. She takes notes
about herd testing.

"It's the way of the future," she says. The future is all around
us, in shiny Babcock testers, in huge signs where the luggage
racks should be:

> *All the money in the bank comes from the soil*
> *Cheap cows are costly cows*
> *Grow two blades of grass where one grew before*
> *Get rid of the old scrub bull*

Sister Crock is restless, she hurries me and Mary along, her
red midi cape flapping around her ample shoulders. The sitting
car awaits. As head of women's subjects, Sister Crock doesn't
want to miss anything. We push on in single file through plant
identification, tobacco, sheep diseases, and honey.

Poultry is next. The poultry car is kept dark to reduce the

anxiety of the birds. It is dimly studded with the beady eyes of hens, pullets, cocks, and roosters. There is no air in poultry, just the acid stench of shit and another smell too: newness, birth, the unfurling and drying of feathers still sappy from the egg. Orange incubation lights sway over the chick cages like giant lampreys. Mr. Ohno, the Japanese chicken sexer, is there, sitting on his haunches in the corner practicing some leather craft. He jerks upright as we enter and then bobs down again in a deep bow. He is immaculate in pinstripe trousers, a long swallowtail jacket, and a silk tie of the deepest scarlet. My eyes settle on his feet, which are, as always, encased in white toe socks worn with heavy wooden clogs. Mr. Ohno's smile is so broad it stretches the part in his brilliantined black hair. He nods formally at Sister Crock and Mary, but stands in front of me.

"Miss Jean. I show you, Miss Jean," he says, taking my hands in his. Then he reaches quickly into one of the wire cages and pulls out a tiny chick.

"Feel he-yah," he says. "He-yah." He guides my fingers over the warm pink rim of the chick's sex, searching for the spine. I think I feel something, the smallest knot of tissue, then Mary giggles and Sister Crock clears her throat noisily and it's gone.

Mr. Ohno snatches the chick away triumphantly. "Ees boy. You feel boy, Miss Jean!"

He bows again and returns the chick to its cage. Sister Crock tells him in her loud, lecturing voice that we are not intending to stop, but are just passing through on our way to the sitting car. He nods at her and bows once more in front of me.

"What number are you, Miss Jean?"

I'm puzzled. I look at Mary for help and she answers for me.

"She twenty-three, Mr. Ohno. Just the right age for a girl, don't you think?"

Mr. Ohno smiles and nods some more. The skin around his eyes folds into tiny crinkles. I would like to touch them. Mr. Ohno is the first Japanese I have ever met. He is small but there is something complete about him. He has been with us for two tours—nearly a whole year. He is a world-famous chicken sexer. His record of five hundred white leghorns in forty-five minutes with 99 percent accuracy and no deaths or injuries has never been bettered.

The soil and cropping wagon is a relief. It has been newly added to the train for our tour into the wheat-growing districts of Victoria. The wagon is glass-roofed—all sunlight and air and swaying plants, a greenhouse on rails. We walk down the aisle as if down the middle of a field parted by God. The wheat in the good field on the left is tall and vigorous, the stems reaching out to touch our skirts; on the right just a few dry sticks poke from the soil.

THE SOIL IS HUNGRY FOR PHOSPHATE—USE SUPERPHOS-PHATE, says the sign. There can be no doubting the magic of it.

Mary Maloney explained superphosphate to me like this: "It's an earth mineral, a powdered earth mineral, the best ever discovered, and it makes you light up."

"How do you mean?"

"Well . . ." Mary's words were unsteady. "I'm just telling what I heard, not what I've seen, but when you touch it in the sack or on the ground it makes you glow like there's a light inside you. Dad heard of a bloke down at Drouin who spread it in the morning and woke up in the night with his hands all alight. They found him in the dam next morning, stiff with cold."

Sister Crock said his death was clearly a case of poor farm hygiene. But I rolled the strange new word around on my tongue—superphosphate, superphosphate, superphosphate. If you drank the water from around the lit-up farmer, or perhaps just a little of the powder in a clean cup mixed with water, would you glow all over? If it lit up your body, would it light up your mind?

Sister Crock slides the door of the sitting car. It is another tunnel of smell. The smell of men. We smile and nod our greetings and take our places on the plush leather seats. A dozen men sit smoking, cross-legged, some still in their white demonstrator's coats. The superintendent is working at his desk.

There are two types of men on the Better-Farming Train—agricultural and railways. Each is then divided again. In railways there are stokers and drivers whom we never see, guards and officials that we do. In agricultural there are stock hands, demonstrators, and experts. Only the demonstrators and experts make it to the sitting car, except for Mr. Ohno, who prefers the company of his chickens, and the new soil and cropping expert, who prefers the company of himself. The stock hands travel in the hay stall, where they play serious card games on the uneven bales.

We have an effect on the men. But not like we have on the animals. The men shut down for a time when we arrive. Their talk drops to a murmur and they draw themselves in, hugging their arms to their bodies, closing off their smell.

"How are your numbers, Sister?" An innocent but foolish question from Mr. Plattfuss.

Sister Crock takes a deep breath, then she's off. Attendances for lecturettes at Marnoo, average weight of babies presented, numbers of primary- and secondary-school girls, quantities of pamphlets and recipes handed out. She quizzes a few of the lingerers after each lecturette and from this has compiled another set of statistics—*miles traveled & mode*. Sister Crock says we can judge the wealth and health of our country by the increasing number of motor cars. But when the heat is rising in our demonstration car the smell is still of warm pony and wet leather. Many children wear the stain of horse sweat between their thighs.

The sitting car rumbles again with discussion. Mary has joined the dairy demonstrators who are talking about mastitis. Mary and I have talked about mastitis late at night in our bunks—Mary hanging above me like the dairy angel, her voice muffled in the small space of our sleeping compartment.

"Dad can tell just by their faces. They'll be walking into the shed of a morning and he'll say, Mary, take this one out, she's got sore . . ."

"Sore what? Come on, what did he say?"

Mary whispers, "*Titties*. I get a basin of warm water and Dettol and sit and massage her udder. Sometimes it's burning, so hot and swollen. I have to be very gentle, kneading like dough. I can tell if I am doing it the right way because she gives this special sort of grunt. Sometimes the kneading frees things up and a big spurt of first milk comes out, all over me."

When Mary talks mastitis my chest buzzes. It is a surging feeling around my nipples. To quiet it I must lay my hands upon my breasts and think cool thoughts.

I notice, whilst Mary talks mastitis with the men in the sitting car, her own hand is flat upon her bodice, not cupping a breast but skirting her throat and down a little where the flesh softens and parts into two.

Mary says I will find love in the sitting car but I am not looking for it. I sit and sew while Mary and the men talk and Sister Crock calculates her statistics. Sewing looks industrious and involving but I can drill stitches while barely looking at my fingers. I sit and sew and listen. I am listening for something important, some piece of knowledge that will take hold of me, that will give me the same certainty of purpose as the men I sit amongst.

I know I won't find knowledge in the women's car. I'm not fooled by Sister Crock's methods—we are merely playing at science, using its language to dress up the drudgery of women's lives. There was no certainty in the lives of the women who gathered in my aunt's front room for fittings and alterations and tea and endless stories of shameful births, wayward children, and disappointment. Women's talk.

Progress is the word that dips and slides through the men's discussions in the sitting car. Men bring progress. They are so sure of progress they measure it constantly—number of acres cleared in a day, bushels of hay cut, pints of milk produced, acres of seed sown, tons of firewood cut. Men measure the activity of progress "per man, per day." Four acres of Mallee scrub can be cleared per man, per day. Although this seems to deny something that even I can see—that all men are different, that some light the way with their ideas and others are merely followers.

Take Mr. Baker, sitting next to me on the banquette, with his thick orange whiskers sprouting at unruly angles. Mr. Baker wants to speak only of pigs. He has on board some prime specimens, which he reminds us of often. His three breeds of pigs, pure Berkshire, middle Yorkshire, and large Yorkshire, are the "triumvirate of future quality." He likes to muse on the numerous crossings and uncrossings that can be achieved among the three breeds and predict what might be produced.

Mr. Talbot, on my other side, talks sheep diseases. He is a little shy. Mary says this is not unusual for a sheep man. Mr. Talbot has a long, thin face and soulful eyes. Sometimes I help him color in his slides of the tissue diseases of sheep. He has a child's pencil case with a beautiful set of colored pencils. I am to use natural colors, he says, lots of reds and pinks. Then I label the drawings in black ink and draw arrows to features of interest. I have colored tuberculosis, actinomycosis, contagious pleuropneumonia, liver fluke, and hydatids.

Then there's the superintendent, sitting stiffly at his desk drafting telegrams to the agriculture minister describing our progress. Sometimes he will give us all an "impromptu lecturette" on our roles as propagandists and the importance of agricultural education in the development of a truly modern society. Most of us have been on the train for several tours—a year or more—but we still listen politely.

Some of the men ask about my sewing. Mr. Baker breaks off from pig talk and points at my lap.

"And what useful item are you making there, Miss Finnegan?"

I hold the lace netting out to him.

"Ah, a veil." His whiskers dip and bob as he speaks. "Do you have a sister getting married?"

"I have no sisters."

Mary covers the marriage terrain for me as we lie on our

bunks. It amuses her so I feign interest. Sister Crock is already snoring loudly in the next compartment. Mary starts with the older, portly men and works down to the more likely. Many of them are damaged, either by the war or by work. Several have lost fingers. Mr. Plattfuss has a glass eye. Mr. Baker has a glass eye *and* an ugly, dragging scar across his cheek where a sharp fencing wire has danced upon him. All of the older men, that is older than thirty, have sun-roughened skin and thinning hair. Mr. Pettergree, the new soil and cropping expert, seems to be some sort of scientific recluse. He never comes to the sitting car and we have seen him only from a distance.

"And what think you of the Asiatic?" Mary asks me with mock formality.

I laugh, but the truth is I think of Mr. Ohno a great deal. I imagine him standing in the poultry car taking off his jacket. He hands it to me so I can study its strange seams and creases. Then I can't help but lift it to my face.

Only one of the men is beautiful—Mr. Kit Collins from horticulture. Mr. Kit Collins has large green eyes and curly hair. He is an expert on the pruning and irrigation of fruit trees. On rest days when the men play cricket in a paddock next to the train, Mr. Kit Collins always switches the ball for an orange, and the batsman always pretends he hasn't noticed until after the orange has been hit and flies mushily through the air.

2

FRANK FINNEGAN'S FRUIT

1915

My dad gave me an orange every day. Each peeling was an exploration—they were all different, on the outside and on the inside too. My dad was an orchardist—*Frank Finnegan's Fruit*. He smelled of soil and oranges just on the turn. His cheeks were gravelly and bits of pith filled out the gaps between his teeth. He sent me to school at four to get me out from under him. I walked down the hill and across the creek, the orange rolling backwards and forwards in my metal case. We had a cat called Abe who walked nearly all of the way with me but he got shy near the road and slunk back home even though I tried to call him across or lead him with a bit of torn-up sandwich.

I had sticky fingers. The books always got dirty. I spilled the ink. My white embroidery square was crumpled and smeary. It said, *Jean Finneg*— I wasn't able to finish it. My hair had knots, but only at the back. First thing each morning we did physical jerks outside by the flagpole. My bonnet flopped in my eyes. I

13

couldn't stand on one leg or stretch up tall like a giraffe without wobbling.

My mother died before my eyes had barely opened, and because of this people liked to touch me and give me things. Most weeks the teacher gave me something from her pocket—a hair slide, a picture of the Baby Jesus all fat and white like a grub, or a piece of chocolate. A special low voice went with the giving and some patting of my arm or head. I thought that was like me with Abe the cat, so I tried to stay still for her and look happy to be petted.

I liked the singing and when the teacher read us a story. I didn't like all the numbers dancing around getting taken in or taken away by the other numbers. I didn't like the spelling words that stayed on the blackboard all week until the test on Friday: *cho-rus, shrap-nel, corps, kha-ki.*

I didn't like it when the teacher split us into boys and girls and we had special talks. Our talks were about being modest and having babies. The teacher showed us a map of Australia and drew a big rectangle inside the middle of it with a ruler.

"See this—all empty. And whose job is it to fill up the empty continent with lovely, healthy babies? It's your job, girls. What an honor. What a privilege . . ."

Then we had to write an essay about duty, but because I was the youngest I was allowed to draw a picture. I drew the middle of Australia filled up with Baby Jesuses. Baby Jesuses covering all the paddocks of all the farms, Baby Jesuses top-to-toeing it across the desert, and one Baby Jesus high up on Ayers Rock with a smiling dingo for company.

The boys' talks were about the war. The war was in England,

the mother country to our country, but the fighting was happening in other places, like France and Turkey.

After school I walked back up the hill and looked for Dad in the sheds. Often he was down at the creek fixing the pump so I went paddling and made dams until it was time for tea. It was my job to butter the bread. Then Dad did the orders or read some books. He was on a quest for knowledge and I was not to disturb him during the quest. Then Abe the cat played the piano. It was all broken down and the white keys were a bit yellow where I had put butter on them to encourage him, but some of the black keys still worked. Abe walked backwards and forwards making his jumbly music. He was four octaves long. He had three tabby legs and one white leg. I liked to watch the patterns of them as they struck the keys.

On Saturdays we went on deliveries right into Melbourne. On the way home we visited my auntie in Hawthorn. She made us tea but we had to sit outside because we were dirty from the cart. On Sundays I had a bath with Dad and we washed our clothes and went walking. We walked every track in the district. Sometimes we followed the creek up into the bush. Once I saw three lyrebirds on the same day but they might have been the same one.

My cat, Abe, went missing on a school day. Dad said he'd probably gone courting but we looked for him in the sheds and in the orchard and under the fruit crates. I walked to school on my own. For physical jerks we walked along a balance beam "graceful like a cheetah." I felt sick. I felt like I'd swallowed a stone and whenever I moved, it scraped at my neck.

I was peeling my orange at lunchtime when I saw Dad talking to the teacher in the doorway to the classroom. His nose was all sunburned and his ears stuck out like the handles on a toby jug. The teacher motioned me over and I heard Dad ask if it was all right for me to come home now because he had a lot on and a bit of help from the nipper wouldn't go astray. The teacher gave him her soft smile and nodded. I got a piggyback up the hill. My hands were orange juice sticky on Dad's shirt but he didn't mind.

Abe was in an apple box on the kitchen table. He was all long and flat—all of him was there but none of him was there. His fur stood up rough and wouldn't sit flat even when I stroked it. His mouth was open a little and the pale pink of his tongue made me gulp. Dad parted the fur on his one white leg to show me the puncture wound from the snake's fangs—two holes an inch apart.

Dad got the shovel and we searched around the sheds and down by the creek. I went along with it but I didn't really want to find the snake. I was frightened, but mainly I didn't want to see the killing.

I thought I saw it—a branch wrapped in muscle flowing over the concrete apron under the pump, but I didn't call out. Instead I complained of being thirsty, of a pain in my eyeball, of needing to pee, so Dad would come away.

We dug a grave for Abe in the orchard.

"All clay, this soil," Dad said. I picked some dandelion heads and put them in the hole, then we went back to get Abe. Dad picked up the box and turned for the kitchen door but stopped suddenly in his tracks.

"Jesus Christ. Jesus H. Christ. He blinked. He bloody blinked."

He put the box down on the kitchen table and I saw it too. A slow, perfect blink. We felt for his heartbeat. There was a faint thud like rocks moving about underwater. Dad was grinning so wide I could see his big yellow side teeth. He ruffled my hair, he picked me up, and we did a jig around the kitchen. "Talk about nine lives," he said. "Talk about nine bloody lives, eh?" Then he walked to town to see Dr. Smurthwaite and get some advice.

Abe didn't move. He hardly breathed—just the occasional blink. I stroked his back until it warmed up, then I did the piano for him.

The book on par-al-y-sis said we had to manage the patient's essential functions and wait for the brainstorm to subside. We trickled sugar water and milk down Abe's throat. We massaged his limbs and bent them backwards and forwards as if he were walking. We breathed into his fetid mouth to expand his lungs. Dad carried him outside and laid him on the dirt. He felt around his tummy and squeezed different bits until some pee trickled out. He was limp. He didn't even purr, but he was still alive in the morning.

The first week after the bite when I walked home from school I thought Abe would be either dead or better, but he just lay in the box. We did the essential functions in the morning and the evening. I drew pictures and propped them up in his box. I drew our house, some orange trees, a fish in the creek, a mouse, a family of mice, the Australian continent covered in mice. Two weeks passed, then two months. I grew an inch. I finished the *Second Schools Reader* but there were no copies of the third reader in the cupboard.

We were being good at the war—especially on the Gallipoli

Peninsula. At school we copied out a notice for our mothers asking them to donate sheets, pillowcases, towels, white shirts, or
frocks for the war. I got to tidy the bookshelf instead. Then we
called out ideas and the teacher wrote a list on the board.

>*How we can earn money for the*
>*State School's Patriotic Fund:*
>*1. Collect eggs.*
>*2. Shift fence posts.*
>*3. Catch leeches for the hospital.*
>*4. Make and sell jam.*
>*5. Sell empty bottles.*
>*6. Catch frogs for the university.*
>*7. Donate birthday money.*
>*8. Catch difficult horses.*
>*9. Donate money for sweets.*

Hazel Meaks said she was going to sell her pet lamb to the
butcher and everyone clapped, then she cried.

I pretended I was sick to avoid eating lamb. I caught three
frogs. When Dad opened my school tin to put the orange in, he
asked what the frogs were for.

"The war."

He nodded. "Good in the trenches, no doubt."

Then one day I walked up the hill and Abe was sitting on the
gatepost washing himself as if he had never been sick. I hadn't
even been thinking about him—I'd been thinking about sub-
traction and how you were meant to know when to borrow a

small number from a bigger number and then to pay it back again. I followed Abe all afternoon. He went to the orchard and the packing sheds and under the house. He went to the stables and fell asleep in the straw. Dad made us pancakes to celebrate but he put orange juice in the mixture and it curdled.

I asked my auntie for scraps of material to take to school and hand in for the war. My auntie made dresses for ladies. I asked her for white scraps or cream scraps so they could be used for bandages.

The first time I saw Dad in green I didn't really see him. The green of his uniform was the same green as the orange trees, but the sleeves were too short so I saw his long wrists and big hands. I saw the sharp bones that stuck out at the sides of his wrists. Sometimes I rubbed these bones on his wrists when I couldn't sleep.

The next time we went to my auntie's she let us into the house. She showed me how she had put up a curtain across part of her sewing room to make another little room. She said it was nice. She said it was quite roomy even.

I couldn't take Abe with me to my auntie's because of the ladies that came around. Anyway, the woken-up Abe was different. He didn't play the piano anymore, he didn't like to be picked up, he had gotten very thin and sometimes when I watched his sinewy back move it made me shudder. He hissed at Dad.

I went to a new school near my aunt's house. At this school the boys made sandbags and the girls knitted socks. My dad wrote first from the training camp at Broadmeadows, where he complained about the badly draining soils, then from France. My dad died in the Battle of Fromelles. In his last letter he said it was a beaut place with lots of churches all ringing out with the sound of bells.

3

THE FOLLY COW

When I sew the veil in the sitting car it is my protector. The men leave me to it. I am the "dark and serious type" with my head bent low over the cloth. "Not a natural smiler," my aunt said. The veil isn't even a veil, just a scrap of curtain netting from the window near my bed. I cut it without taking the rail down. It left the netting a good foot short of the windowsill, but my aunt didn't notice. Or perhaps she noticed after I'd left. I didn't take much else. Just a scrap from my old life to take into the new.

At first I thought I would just fill in the holes. But it became something else. Forms took shape that I hadn't planned, lines and whirls darted through the netting leaving bright trails of color. Stitches rose and stretched and fell in jagged rays from their source.

When I sew the veil in public I keep it tightly tucked into my lap, busy on one small area. Later, when I sit on my bunk and inspect the work, I am often amazed. It seems I have stitched the very shape of the conversation in the sitting car. The heat of it,

21

the dips and lulls, the opinions and arguments, the conflict between the railway's men and the agriculture men, it is all there
in wandering thread.

In my lecturettes I say that sewing is about completing the
circle. I draw a circle on my blackboard and then turn to them
and say, "You see, that's all a stitch is, any stitch, it's just a circle.
Around and around it goes. A well-made stitch doesn't reveal
where it was started or how it was tied off, it just is."

I teach them sheeting, kitchen linen, blouses, the V-neck,
the drop waist, riding pants, men's shirting. I am qualified to
teach infant garments but Sister Crock has told me firmly that
she will speak on all aspects of baby care and management. I
have been asked to teach work garments, practical garments,
and this is what I do, but the questions are always about other
things.

The women will listen with great patience to my lecturette
and then ask me about something entirely different. They ask
me about Chinese collars and pleats and self-knotting scarves—
impractical garments. And at every siding there is always one
woman who will wait until everyone has left to shyly show me
her embroidery. Lavender is very popular. I admire tea cloths
shiny with sickly purple and mint green.

I suggest they sew things they see around them. Perhaps
wheat heads or gum tree blossom? I produce samplers from my
college days: the whirring spokes of a bicycle wheel, a fatly
coiled tiger snake, a cloth stitched with the word for love in ten
different languages. The women look with interest and surprise.
I do not tell of the consternation these pieces caused the college
embroidery instructor. Now I am the teacher.

"What about your husband?" I say. "Perhaps you can capture his image, a little each evening when he comes in." Sometimes they are barely more than schoolgirls, they giggle and blush. I admire the women that I teach. They are not like me in the sitting car, a shy spectator. They are truly within their lives, working in partnership with their husbands for the good of each other.

If we repeat this tour next year I wonder if they will return and bring their new work to show me. If just one woman at each stop brought a rough-stitched sampler of her husband, we would have a gallery. I could stitch them together into a massive quilt—"the beloved farmers of Victoria, caught at rest, by their wives."

Sister Crock was here first (I have heard the men joke about the "maiden" on the maiden journey). Mary Maloney came next, then me. When I was appointed I made an agreement with Mary. She was to improve my cooking and I was to correct her sewing, but it hasn't worked out like that at all.

When we are not lecturing, or preparing, or traveling in the sitting car, we roam the train together. We have attended some of the lecturettes and watched all of the demonstrations. Our favorite is the "detraining of stock." As soon as we arrive at a stop the stock hands don their white coats and climb through the slats into the animal wagons. Mr. Plattfuss, the head of stock, makes an announcement. He holds a loud-hailer in one hand and waves theatrically with the other. *Bang,* the ramp doors of the wagons are let down all at once and the stock is walked out. The biggest bulls come first, blinking into the bright light. An almost continuous line of animals follows, all of them stiff-legged, not yet adjusted to solid ground after the journey.

Big crowds gather for the detraining. They push forward towards the train only to be barked at by Mr. Plattfuss, whose handlebar mustache neatly mimics the curve of the loud-hailer he holds to his mouth.

"Stand back. Stand back. Make way for some of the finest animals in the nation."

Mr. Plattfuss announces the name of each beast as it descends the ramp. There are many different breeds of sheep and goats but most attention is paid to the cattle. The cows shine in their loveliness, different colors and shapes. Some are sweetly pretty, others are exotic with deeply set eyes behind dark, heavy lashes.

Mr. Plattfuss tugs at his too-tight white coat and reels off statistics about calving rates and butterfat production. He calls an elegant Friesian the pride of her breed. He says a Red Poll is the cow of the future.

Then the folly cow is led out, always last. She is just an ordinary cow. Mary says she is actually quite a good example of an ordinary cow. Mr. Plattfuss can't wait. The cow is still on the ramp and he is deriding her.

"This, gentlemen," he says, "is the cow of the past. A plain scrub cow with no particular parentage. Her butterfat production is poor but she still eats the same as her better sisters. You must weed out these poor producers. She is the folly cow—it is your own folly to keep wasting fodder on her."

The folly cow blinks and bends her big knees awkwardly. As if on cue she loses her footing on the ramp and slips over the last rung. A young stock attendant, the very youngest (no one wants to lead the folly cow), walks her away.

Mary shakes her head angrily and says it is time for some cooking. I help her mix up a batch of rough, crumbly pastry. She fills it with black treacle. We bake treacle pie for the folly cow and feed her in the evenings after all the crowds have left. The treacle is doing her coat wonders; she glistens with good health.

"Hello, my sweet," we say, like she is a child. Mary holds the pie as she bites through the crust and uses her fat pink tongue to scoop up the treacle. "Hello, my lovely Folly." She smells glorious, of warm fur and milk and sweet treacle. Mary is dismissive of the fancy breeds. She says when the drought strikes and times are hard you need a good-doer—you need an honest and practical animal that will make the best of what's on offer. She could have been describing herself.

Mr. Ohno has seen us tending Folly. At Golden Square he walked off into the hills and picked her a thick sward of purple pasture. Mary had to explain that it was Paterson's Curse—a highly toxic weed causing spontaneous calf abortion. She had to mime some of the difficult words and it was hard to tell if he understood.

Mr. Ohno likes animals and he is easy with children. At Bendigo I watched from the carriage window as he teased two small farm boys holding a Shetland pony on a length of dirty clothesline.

"Is kangaloo?" Mr. Ohno asked them, mock-serious with his hands in his pockets. The little boys doubled over with laughter, banging into each other and holding their hands across their stomachs.

"Oh. Is not kangaloo?"

Mr. Ohno asked the boys their names and numbers and offered them a few coins for a ride of their charge. The Shetland pony, true to form, was hugely fat. Mr. Ohno hoisted himself up as if mounting a beer barrel, his slim legs splayed wide around the pony's swollen belly. The ensemble was incongruous but somehow also stylish. Mr. Ohno's swallowtail jacket looked like a smart riding coat and his black hair could have passed for a shiny helmet. And they were oddly in proportion.

One of the boys slapped the pony over the rump and it lurched into a reluctant trot. Mr. Ohno grabbed a hank of mane with one hand and put the other out for balance. Then he looked across at the train, turned his head and scanned the carriages, looking in at the windows. He was smiling a proud smile and I realized he was riding the pony for me.

4

A Lecturette on Good Soil Husbandry

Women don't generally attend farming lecturettes but Mary's
story has sparked my interest in superphosphate. There are big
crowds at Warracknabeal so a marquee is erected alongside the
train. I sit in the last row with a flap of canvas lifting against my
back. The men in front of me are wearing their hats so my view
is blocked. I can't see Mr. Pettergree standing at the front but
the murmuring of the men stops as soon as he starts to talk. He
has an English country accent—each sentence carried by the
same singsong rhythm—and no regard for his *h*'s. There is another quality too—a certain pitch or urgency.

"Imagine you want to kill your dog—do you cut off its paw
and then wait?" The men shift a little in their seats.

"Do you watch the thing limp behind you and bleed and
howl? Of course not. You shoot it outright."

He pauses.

"Then why, I ask you, do we do it to trees? You ringbark a
tree today it'll die sure enough, but it could still be standing
there haunting you in twenty years' time. You can't farm prop-

27

erly with paddocks full of dead wood. Your first duty as farmers is to completely clear the land. Once you've got nothing between yourself and the soil—that's the time for agriculture."

The men nod. There are a few faint *hear-hears*.

"You men might think you know how to farm, but you know nothing. You know nothing because you are always looking in the wrong place. You're watching at the ears of your corn or the heads of your wheat and forgetting the most important component of the whole equation—the soil. For the past seven years I have studied the soils of Victoria and I have no hesitation in telling you that your soil—the soil of the Mallee—is the poorest. You are the men with the greatest challenge of all. Your soil is barely more than sand. Leave it without crop cover and it'll up and blow back to the seaside. Remember that the soil is a living organism. If you want to feed yourself, you must feed the soil. You have to get to know your soil. Gentlemen, you have to watch it and touch it. You have to taste it."

There is a pause; the audience shuffle in their seats and look about uncomfortably. I stand up to get a better view. The new soil and cropping expert, Mr. Pettergree, is kneeling next to the lectern as if he is praying, his white laboratory coat bunching and folding at his thighs. He digs into the dirt with a penknife, extracts a clod, and rolls it in his hand like tobacco. Then he stands. Slowly and with great deliberation he lifts the soil to his mouth and licks. I see his tongue flick over the dirt; all the while his eyes look straight ahead, holding the gaze of the audience.

He motions for the men to copy him. A few do, then they shake their heads and spit with distaste. But there is little time to ponder. Mr. Pettergree resumes his spiel. He talks rapidly, leaping from one subject to the next. He is taking us on a journey starting at the very beginning of the earth. He talks of carboniferous sands dotted with the fossilized bones of ancient creatures; he talks of Australia's inland sea. He describes our soils as the relics of ancient history—the red-brown earths, red clays, brownish sands, stony downs, desert loams, black-cracking clays, soft-red soils, and the poorest soils of all, the skeletals.

He explains the moral and patriotic duty of the farmer who comes across a ruined soil to repair it, and he shows us how. He shows us superphosphate.

All of the audience is on their feet now, but the man in front of me moves a little so I get a better view. Mr. Pettergree is sorting through some papers at the lectern. He is around thirty, not tall, but strongly built. His chest, in a gray serge suit, juts out noticeably at the front. He has dark, coppery red hair. He is sweating. Strong and red, this is the sense I get of him—a man flushed with purpose.

Mr. Pettergree has only recently joined the train and I have never seen him in the sitting car. I have noticed him, though. I watched him recently through the window while we were stopped for water at a small siding. He walked some distance into a paddock and dug a hole with a handpick. As he was walking back to the train I saw several bulging calico bags threaded through his belt. I think he was sampling the soil. I smiled to myself, as I thought he was taking a souvenir from the route of the journey in the same way Mary collects the posters we send ahead to each station advertising our arrival. But I was wrong. Mr. Pettergree wasn't collecting out of sentiment, he was collecting for knowledge. He is not just a man who asks questions but a man with answers.

Mr. Pettergree hands around two photographs and waits while they are passed from man to man, row to row. When they reach the back the young farmer next to me is confused. Should he give me the photographs, or keep holding them? He passes them to me abruptly, saving himself from having to walk to the front and return them. The first photograph shows a stubbly paddock with a few poor-looking sticks of wheat. The second a lush and healthy stand of tall, shiny stalks. It would be easy to say the photographs were simply taken on different farms, except for the sign that appears in both. PETTERGREE'S SUPER-PHOSPHATE TRIAL, it says, in black paint on a white timber cross.

Mr. Pettergree drags a heavy sack from under the lecture table to show us. The men crane their necks to see as he digs his hands into the sack and holds two great handfuls aloft—an offering. I am surprised it is just a powder, pale and chalky.

"This—*this* is farmers' gold," he says. "Australia's soils are old men—this is the tonic that will bring back their youth."

The lecturette is over. The men leave the benches and Mr. Pettergree starts to pack his equipment away. I sit and watch him for a minute and then get up to return the photographs. He hears me walking towards him down the aisle between the benches and looks up. He frowns a little. He is clearly surprised to see a woman at his lecturette. I hold the photographs out to him. "Here. These are yours."

He stares at me fixedly. He is staring at my mouth. I touch my lips, brush the grains of soil away, and smile nervously.

"Hello, Mr. Pettergree from soil. I am Miss Finnegan from sewing."

I have learned this about Mr. Pettergree: he does not smoke; he is from Yorkshire; he did night classes at Melbourne University while working in an insurance office by day; he has spent the past seven years at the Rutherglen Research Station; he knows more about soil than any man in Victoria. I start to notice him. I notice how he hangs back when collecting his sandwiches so we arrive at the lunch table together. He favors egg and lettuce. I notice that he often arrives late when a local dignitary is making the welcome speech and sidles slowly through the crowd until he is standing behind me. But it is Mary who uncovers something interesting. She asks the stock hands about him and after some questioning and some fruitcake and more questioning and a jam sponge, they finally tell her what Mr. Pettergree does of an evening.

They call him "the taster." They say he can identify any place in the state of Victoria just by the taste of its soil. The stock hands run the racket. They put out the word from station to station, seeking the type of men to take such a gamble. They spell out the rules—bring a handful of soil wrapped in newspaper or a handkerchief and bring a pound. Double or nothing.

It happens in the evening, after the displays have been packed away and the superintendent has been driven into town to the best hotel. The men gather on the tracks at the front of the train. They light a fire in a drum and share a beer. They wait for the taster. When he is ready he walks out of the dark and takes a position near the fire. He needs the light to see the sample and a little warm water to mix with it before he tastes. He doesn't drink the beer. He isn't part of the jostling or backslapping or money talk. He comes, tastes, and leaves, taking half of each stake with him. The stock hands pool the rest, buying beer and sometimes spirits, funding their poker marathons, and, in the bigger towns, visiting the tabbies. The stock hands often theorize about what Pettergree does with the money—send it back to the old country to a sweetheart, buy gold, pay off his debts? . . . In more drunken moments they say he eats it and tastes every place in Australia it has been, ending up back at the mint.

The larking stops as soon as the taster arrives. He takes the sample, lifts it to his tongue, closes his eyes, considers, spits.

"Rupanyup. Closer to Minyip, maybe, but not far off."

The sample bringer is agog. The odds had looked good—what man could match a soil to its location by taste alone? The stock hands take his money and give him a beer in consolation.

The taster rarely fails. Sometimes tricks are played. At Avoca, where he was expecting the gravelly duplexes of the Pyrenees, a Gippsland black loam was presented. The sample bringer, a battered-looking laborer with ill-fitting false teeth and a nasty sneer, insisted the sample came from the Avoca football ground. The taster knew the truth before the soil touched his tongue. The laborer demanded his winnings, his voice rising to a whining falsetto, but his crookedness was well known amongst the crowd.

"Tell the truth, Frogley, you bloody liar."

"Neville bloody Frogley. You couldn't lie straight in your own bed."

Finally he admitted that, yes, he had taken a trip to Leongatha and brought back the soil packed around some fish he'd caught in the river. . . .

"The Bass River?" Pettergree asked.

The laborer was silent for a minute then exploded with frustration. "Yes, the bloody Bass River." He looked at the men gathered around him and kicked at the ground with his boot.

"Strewth, it's only soil."

5

THE HONEY CAR

We have stopped for a few days' rest at a siding near Dimboola. The animals are released into paddocks alongside the railway line and we are driven into town to buy supplies. The mayor and his wife take some of the train's senior men and all three of its women on a tour of the town hall and a new cricket ground. I picnic with Mary at Woraigworm Station and we look for Mallee fowl, a strange scientific bird that builds a nest like an oven and bakes its precious eggs into life. The people of Dimboola bring us their produce: bags of flour, a watermelon large enough to sit on, some beehives ripe for extraction.

I write up my notes and sort through my samples and supplies. I have twenty-one half-finished turn-back collars. One for each town we have visited. I am walking alongside the train, checking to see if Folly is getting her fair share of the pasture, when a window slides up and Robert Pettergree calls down to me from the honey car.

"Come up here," he says. "The apiarists are at the pub and these hives need doing before they candy."

He hoists me up into the car by the plump of my arm. It is hot and dark inside—the shutters are drawn to calm the bees. He places a knife in my hand; its bone handle radiates heat.

"Here," he says, "like this."

He hands me a wooden frame strung with a fine-gauge wire mesh. Each tiny square is filled with waxy honey. I sluice the wire with the hot knife. The wax melts. Honey drips slowly, brightly, through the mesh into the tub of the extractor. It is so hot in the honey car. I plunge the knife into a jug of boiling water to clean it. The stove at the end of the car crackles, a kettle steaming on top of it.

"Here," he says. "Here." He is moving quickly, going outside opening hive boxes, removing frames, bringing them to me. Each frame brings a few bees with it. Slow, sad bees stuck amongst the honey and the wax. Slow bees crushed between the frames. Slow bees in my hair and on my wrists.

I am sweating. Sweat slides from my face and throat and mixes with the honey. There is honey on my cheeks, my fingers, my dress, on the toes of my shoes.

He tends the fire and refills the knife jug with boiling water. His part of the job is done. He doesn't thank me. He doesn't offer to help. He just stands and watches as I sluice the last of the frames.

"I did a bit of bee work with my uncle. In the old country."

I nod. My arms ache with the weight of the frames.

"It's hot in here."

I nod again. Then he takes off his shirt, pulling it over his head, the buttons still done up. It is so tender a thing to see—his face hidden in the cotton like a boy's.

I watch him as he takes a cup of water, drinks, and splashes it onto his head and chest. Then he is behind me, sprinkling water over me, flicking it through his fingers. I lean back towards him. He paints me with water, his thick finger dipping into the cup then tracing my forehead and the curve of my jaw.

There is a sense of everything crumbling and swirling.

"Go on," he says. "You're not finished."

So I stand with him behind me and drag the knife over the last frame again. But I am weak with it. Honey is splashing and dripping, missing the extractor. He is wetting my arms, pushing his fingers up under my sleeves, wetting my skin, pushing higher, searching out the join between arm and body.

What happens next? I can hardly say . . . but the knife and the frame are gone and I am taking off my dress, arms reaching over my head like him, and letting it fall to the floor of the car into the water and honey.

Then there is this moment—one still moment—when he watches me but does not move and I could almost have felt foolish but for drowsiness from the heat. So I busy my hands with undressing, shoes, stockings, slip, and go to him with my head bowed.

Then he is touching me. From my fingers up to my shoulders, down my legs and up again, across my breasts, licking the fine hairs that snake down my belly, stopping to part my sex with his tongue.

His clothes are with mine on the floor and then we are on top of them. He is biting my mouth, dragging and sucking my lips, folding them in his. His tongue is strong and urgent. He grips my breasts hard in his hands, the flesh spilling between his fingers. He is drawing out my nipples in his mouth, then letting them fall, stunned. He is grinding his penis into the flesh of my belly. Hard flesh into soft. He is working at me, pushing at me, his toenails scraping at my calves. It hurts, it is almost pain. He is moaning and keening and straining and then shuddering and suddenly still. His chest feels hard and sharp so I push his shoulder and he moves to the side. There is the sound of skin unsticking.

Then I lie there with him, alight and dripping, until I can take myself away and make it right alone.

Because of the train we are coming together at a gallop. It's different for people who meet on open ground: in a house, on the street, in town. They have the chance to skirt around, to evade, to see each other from different angles, to turn a corner and claim more time. When I conspire to meet Robert Pettergree on the Better-Farming Train, we must walk towards each other down the aisle. If the train is moving we walk with a wide-legged gait for added balance so it looks like we are wading towards each other, a thick sea pulling about our legs.

We meet in the soil and cropping wagon, where he tends his miniature fields. It is not gardening, it is clearly science. He weighs and measures each additive—water, nitrogenous fertilizer, phosphate, potassic fertilizer—and applies them gravely. We sit together on the narrow bench between the rows of wheat while he records his observations in his notebook. The glass louvers on the sides of the wagon are open and it is often windy and noisy. Even when the train is not moving the wind will push the wheat, teasing it, until it sways forward in a pulse. The sun

38

beats through the glass roof so it is almost like sitting in a real paddock, except that we are moving and there is a large sign above our heads: SUPERPHOSPHATE IS THE MANURE OF BIRDS FROM PACIFIC OCEAN ISLANDS.

I measure the wheat. He grows the very best of varieties: *Ghurka, Currawa,* and *Baldmin* are smooth and golden bronze. The strong bearded heads of the *Nabawa* brush my face as I lean to reach its roots. There are native grasses too, clearly poorer in comparison. Wallaby grass, *Amphibromus nervosus*—and it looks nervous indeed, thin stems all elbowed and bent about. Its heads are tiny silky spikelets; they disintegrate between my fingers, leaving traces of skeleton filigree in the air. It would take a day to collect a thimbleful and then a farmer's boot would surely crush it dead. Robert feeds it no additives; he says it just grows, endlessly, everywhere, wallabies spreading the seeds. I imagine they carry it caught in their fur, shaking it off as they bounce, or perhaps grooming it out of each other like monkeys.

Robert explains scientific replication to me. "These plots are like a bathtub, Jean, and there's a great ocean out there, just look at it, stretching for miles. Everything I do in here, small-scale, I could do out there. Imagine the poor soil of the Mallee chemically fertilized to produce at its utmost capacity. Imagine wagonloads of superphosphate being transformed into a train-load of wheat. Imagine, Jean, the harsh backblocks of the Mallee becoming the breadbasket of the nation. What greater challenge could a man have?"

The word *bread* hovers. I wish I'd spent more time watching Mary. I've never been good at baking.

Robert picks a wheat head and dissects it with his scalpel. It is fleshy and tightly packed. I'm surprised at the moistness of it and the strong smell of earth.

It seems to me Robert is a transformer in the same way that Mary is, and that it really is a question of scale. Mary takes the flesh of an animal, or grain from the ground, something raw and unappealing, and makes it into an attractive and flavorsome meal. Robert can turn superphosphate into wheat. Robert's achievements are credited because they are so visible. We gawp at his plants day after day while Mary's apple pie is consumed in minutes.

Mary is hungry for information about Robert's background, but I have little to share. We meet, tend the plants, and he talks about science. Often he doesn't address the talk at me but at the rows of wheat around us. It is hard to keep Mary's interest.

"We touched. Just a little . . ."

"Did he kiss you, Jeanie? Tell. Tell me everything."

"No, it was just the train. You know, we just sort of crashed into one another."

Mary smiles. "I bet he did it on purpose."

I'm perplexed. "But he said sorry."

I can tell that Mary doesn't wholly approve. That she considers Robert odd—a boffin, a cold fish. He certainly hasn't used any of the standard techniques of wooing and seduction. We have barely touched at all since the honey car. When the train does throw us together, accidentally, he could steady me, but instead he reaches for the roof of the carriage and I'm left flailing, embarrassed by my outstretched arms.

We spend three days at Jeparit. The train has been skirting the edge of the Mallee but now we are truly within it. The sky seems suddenly to widen and deepen. The country appears uninhabited until we reach the station, where every farmer in the district, every child at the local school, every shopkeeper and every day laborer, is waiting for us. The women have swarmed into the cookery car. They wear their best clothes and Sister Crock is quite overcome with the smell of mothballs. Nothing is white in Jeparit. The water is hard and rusty and they wear its color—streaky orange. The wheat, too, suffers from rust. The farmers seek out Robert urgently. They bring bouquets of diseased wheat for him to examine. I have no doubt that he can help them.

Sorry. He sent me a message, via a stock hand, as I helped Mary to clean her pots; she'd burned the jam, again. *Sorry, Jean, can I see you tonight?*

Even after dark the soil and cropping wagon is full. Anxious farmers file through by lamplight, stopping to exclaim at the *Nabawa* and insist some magic has been worked on it. So we meet, for once, on open ground. Robert holds the fencing wires apart for me and we walk into a paddock next to the train. We walk side by side and I notice the solid set of his neck, the breadth of him.

The paddock is empty except for a few dried-up thistles. We walk to the middle and stop. The train glows behind us. Robert takes a slim parcel from his coat.

"You might like to read this, Jean."

His hands guide mine to the page, where I can just make out his name and the title of the article: "Everyman's Rules for Scientific Living. By Robert L. Pettergree, Department of Agriculture."

"I've been working on it for some time. I think it makes clear how things could be. What I—" he stumbles "—what *we* . . . could do."

I turn the journal over in my hands and flick through the neat, typewritten pages.

"There is something else too. I sent away for it."

He pulls a tiny box covered in dark velvet from his pocket then he quickly takes my shoulders and turns me around.

"Shut your eyes."

I can feel the heat of him through my dress. His arms are firm around me and I have a sudden giddy recollection of playing cricket in the orchard with my father. I stood under the strong ledge of his body, our hands laced together around the bat. He smelled of orange peel.

Robert fumbles with the box and reaches for my hand.

"I'm not sure which finger you wear it on."

The metal is cool. I blink with surprise at the gift on my finger. It is a silver thimble. A perfect silver cap finely etched with a pattern of small wheat heads and notched on the top to push off or receive a needle. A thimble is a practical and appropriate gift for a woman—for a sewing instructress—and I know I will keep it forever.

The real gift is some papers inside the agricultural journal. I find them later, as I am meant to. Mortgage papers and a map of a farm at Wycheproof in Robert's hand. The paddocks are neatly drawn with the fences marked in green pencil. The farm is oddly shaped, as one of its long boundaries is a river. He has drawn only one bank of the river with its many twists and bends, but not the other. I guess it will be wide, perhaps with an island in the channel for ducks and swans.

The paddocks are all named, after people or purpose. Gurney's, Dump, Horse, Smith's, Timber, Wether's, Melville's, Back,

Dam, and House. The house paddock is smallish and square but there is no indication of an actual house. I look at the map for some time before I notice something else in the house paddock: the letter *J.* It is quite faint and looks to have been written recently, almost as an afterthought.

> *Everyman's Rules for Scientific Living*
> *By Robert L. Pettergree, Department of Agriculture*
> 1. CONTRIBUTE TO SOCIETY FOR THE ACHIEVEMENT OF MUTUAL BENEFITS.
> 2. THE ONLY TRUE FOUNDATION IS A FACT.
> 3. KEEP UP-TO-DATE.
> 4. AVOID MAWKISH CONSIDERATION OF HISTORY AND RELIGION.
> 5. KEEP THE MIND FLEXIBLE THROUGH THE DEVELOPMENT AND TESTING OF NEW HYPOTHESES.
> 6. CULTIVATE THE COMPANY OF WISER MEN— MEN WHO ARE STICKERS—NOT SHIRKERS.
> 7. DISSEMINATE. THE LABORS AND ACHIEVEMENTS OF MEN OF SCIENCE MUST BECOME THE PERMANENT POSSESSION OF MANY.
> 8. BRING SCIENCE INTO THE HOME.

> *Victorian Department of Agriculture Journal,* May 1934

This short and surprising article—really just a list—appears on page 33 of the *Agriculture Journal.* Before it is a technical paper on the use of copper sulfate by potato farmers and after it several pages of entomological drawings. It is unexpected, unanticipated. I don't know what to make of it so I seek advice.

What Sister Crock says about Robert's article: "A man with a desire for exactitude is a man worth noting." She says this in a kindly way—over the tops of her glasses. Sister Crock is busy preparing her own articles for the *Agriculture Journal*, on the model modern baby. She argues that modern women, and modern rural women in particular, are deficient in their natural capacity for their domestic responsibilities, including motherhood. Sister Crock believes that the modern human mother lacks the strength of instinct to be found in animals. She is producing three related articles: "Mother's Duty to Her Baby," "Milk and the Baby," and "Errors of Maternity."

What Mary Maloney says about Robert's article: "Look, Jean, what they believe in is important—I wouldn't choose a man who has no pride in his work, but perhaps in the end it doesn't matter so much. Do you want to live with someone who thinks they know the answers, or spend your life trying to find them out together? Then there's love—and there's dancing. Now, have you ever seen him dance?"

What the superintendent says about Robert's article: "Mr. Pettergree is a scientist of essentially sound thinking but someone liable to get a little carried away. In future I would like all articles submitted to the *Agriculture Journal* to be approved by me."

What Mr. Baker says about Robert's article, while eating a bacon sandwich: "Mawkish? Religion mawkish? Piffle. Did you see the article on diets for the lactating sow? Now that's worth a read, Miss Finnegan."

What Mr. Plattfuss says about Robert's article while spit-polishing his loud-hailer: "Rules like that are all right for a plant man. In my mind that's the difference between a plant man and an animal man. An animal man isn't going to come up with concrete rules for living and doing because there's no point. With animals everything's always changing. An animal man is looking after something with a heart inside of it and you can't go living by rules when there's a heart involved."

I wonder what Mr. Ohno would make of "Everyman's Rules for Scientific Living." And whether he has some sort of motto or list of his own.

When I spread my sewing out on my bunk each evening there is always one section that catches my eye. One small section where everything is somehow concentrated and clear. When I read Robert's article it is the second rule that stands out for me: The only true foundation is a fact. It is a fact that I have lain naked with Robert Pettergree on the floor of the honey car. It is a fact that I see him lifting his arms and taking off his shirt over and over again in my mind—that I go to sleep at night both soothed and excited by the slow lifting of white cotton and his body being revealed beneath it. These private facts—that I don't share, even with Mary—are my foundation.

6

THREE INCIDENTS AT JEPARIT

Jeparit is memorable for other reasons too. The first is Mr. Ohno's birthday. Mary bakes a pineapple upside-down cake for Mr. Ohno and goes to collect him from poultry. We wait in the sitting car. Everyone is there, even Robert. A few minutes pass then Mary slides the door open and encourages Mr. Ohno through. He takes his place in front of the cake on the superintendent's desk and we sing "Happy Birthday." Mary hands Mr. Ohno the knife and he takes it with a bow, but he doesn't cut the cake. He clears his throat and sings his own version of "Happy Birthday," in a high, serious wail. We stand politely to attention except for Mr. Kit Collins, who is stifling a laugh. As soon as the song is over we clap. Mr. Ohno bows again but still he does not cut the cake. He stands quite still holding the knife and seems overcome with emotion.

"Anyone for hari-kari?" Mr. Talbot whispers, but it is heard by all.

Mr. Ohno looks confused. So I step forward, take his hand in mine, and help him to mark out the slices.

"Who's for cake?"

There is one slice remaining at the end. Robert's slice. He left abruptly, just after I took Mr. Ohno's hand.

Jeparit is also the place where Mr. Talbot from sheep gets into trouble. The superintendent has received a letter of complaint about one of Mr. Talbot's herd management and husbandry lecturettes. The writer, a Mr. Frank Edgcumbe, sheep farmer from Cope Cope, considers Mr. Talbot's comparisons between the undesirability of breeding between cretins and breeding between inferior sheep distasteful and offensive.

Mr. Talbot is deeply hurt. His quiet manner is even more subdued. We are all summoned to the sitting car to "clear up" the matter. I sit wedged between Robert and Sister Crock on one of the long velvet banquettes while Mr. Talbot paces the aisle giving us an abridged version of his spiel. He coughs nervously when he reaches the contentious bit. Robert shifts on the seat next to me. Robert thinks this is a circus—that a farmer's complaints to a scientist are not worth the time of day, that the superintendent should be allowing the train's experts to spend time on research, not just demonstration. Robert's thigh sits alongside mine. I can feel his heat seeping through the cloth of his trousers, through my dress and stockings, deep into my skin. My face is flushed. I look down. It is perplexing that my mind can conjure such intimate pictures of Robert's body while my eyes are firmly fixed on Sister Crock's ankles.

Mr. Talbot continues: "The rational management of breeding amongst stock can be quite simply compared to the rational management of human sexual behavior leading to an improved and efficient human race. A healthy and vigorous sexual union, and I of course mean here *licit* sex—taking place in marriage—is as beneficial to the farm family and the nation as the healthy and appropriate union of well-chosen stock in the joining paddock.

"The opposite, the need to control reproduction between the *illicit* or inappropriate, is just as true. Let me quote from the *Adelaide Mail*: 'Restraint upon propagation of the species by individuals who are afflicted by serious physical or mental infirmities is required. The recognition by persons so afflicted of the necessity for restraint is, we need hardly say, the highest form of patriotism.'

"So, my dear friends and patriots, I conclude by saying, don't put your prize ram with the old ewes from up the back. What you'll get out of it won't take you anywhere. Think about breeding. Think about the traits and characteristics you want to promote, and plan your breeding programs with them in mind."

It doesn't seem appropriate to clap. Although I have noticed some farmers do clap after a lecturette and the women often clap when Mary pulls something high and spicy from the oven.

Mr. Talbot ventures a smile at his audience, but the superintendent rises from his desk and quickly removes it.

"What were you thinking of, Mr. Talbot, to come up with such notions? Are these your ideas or someone else's?"

Mr. Talbot looks about blankly. His gaze settles on Robert and he seems to gain a little focus.

"The *thing is*, Superintendent, that country people don't understand metaphor and so—"

The superintendent interrupts. He says the *thing is* that the Edgcumbes have a nineteen-year-old cretinous son whose head, instead of being filled with brains, leaks watery fluid. The son has not left the house since birth as he wears a turban of bed-sheets to protect his soft, damp noggin. According to the Edg-cumbes he is a fine vegetable sculptor and an able draughts player and they invite Mr. Talbot, or in fact any of the lecturers from the Better-Farming Train, to visit and play a game with him sometime.

The superintendent reminds us all of the influence that we have within the districts that we visit and asks us to revisit our lectures. He suggests we ask ourselves regularly, "Am I following the correct line?" and "Am I providing the best possible exam-ple?" He shares his favorite aphorism: "A thoroughbred doesn't need much whipping. He does his best—do you?"

Mr. G. R. (George Reid) Talbot is an acknowledged expert in sheep breeding. His Talbot Scale of Sheep Semen has been adopted across Australia.

TALBOT SEMEN SCALE

Classification	Approx. no. of sperm in millions per cc
Thick-creamy	More than 3,000
Creamy	2,000–3,000
Milky	500–2,000
Cloudy	Less than 500
Clear	Insignificant

Mr. Talbot developed his useful scale after testing the semen of over 1,800 rams. Talbot's major scientific breakthrough was in sperm collection. He constructed a lifelike artificial ewe vagina and developed considerable skill in teaching his test rams to serve it.

On the outskirts of Jeparit I have my first preparation for married life. Robert teaches me the Principles of Experimentation. It is a psychophysical experiment. We have the cookery car to ourselves—Sister Crock is preparing lesson plans in the sitting car and Mary has made herself scarce.

1. STATEMENT OF EXPERIMENT

A person (me) claims that on tasting a cup of tea she can tell whether the milk or the tea was added to the cup first. Robert mixes eight cups of tea, four in one way and four in the other, and presents them in random order (we have only six cups so he uses the gravy boat and milk jug to make up numbers). Random order, surprisingly, is not something that can be left to the human mind but must be achieved by the actual manipulation of physical apparatus. Robert uses dice but says cards or a roulette wheel is just as effective. A published collection of random sampling numbers is his preferred method but we don't have one to hand.

2. INTERPRETATION AND REASONING

Before actually conducting the experiment it is necessary to have anticipated the range of possible results, and to have decided without ambiguity the interpretation that shall be placed upon them.

Mary would call this "talking it out." After an evening in the sitting car, or after a dinner dance in town, we sit together on our bunks, peeling off our stockings, rubbing our feet, and going over things. We decide what was meant by the things that were said and done and forecast future developments. What interpretation should we put upon Mr. Plattfuss partnering Sister Crock in several of the slower numbers?

3. PERMUTATIONS AND COMBINATIONS

There are seventy ways of choosing a group of four objects out of eight. A person (a cretin perhaps) who has no discrimination would in fact divide the eight cups correctly into two sets of four in one trial out of seventy. The odds could be made much higher by enlarging the experiment (more cups of tea, if available). If the experiment were smaller it would give odds so low that the results could be ascribed to pure chance.

4. THE TEST OF SIGNIFICANCE

"But it is possible that the very first time I tasted the cups I could *accidentally* choose them correctly, even if I wasn't concentrating—even perhaps if I was trying on purpose to get it wrong."

"Why would you do that, Jean?"

"I don't know, I can't really explain. I'm just supposing."

"That would be sabotage. There's no point in going on if you're going to be like that."

He has a nervous habit of using his finger to trace the crease from his nose to his mouth. I must have seen him do it many times before but this is the first time I notice it. He does it when he is perturbed, when things aren't going to plan. He does it, I think, to comfort himself.

"Sorry. Go on. Please go on."

"It is standard for experimenters to take five percent as a test of significance, in the sense that they are prepared to ignore all results which fail to reach this standard and to eliminate from further discussion the fluctuations which chance introduces into their experimental results. Do you understand that?"

"Yes, of course. I understand."

5. STATISTICAL ANALYSIS

I can choose three cups right and one cup wrong in sixteen ways.

I can choose two cups right and two wrong in thirty-six ways.

I can choose one cup right and three cups wrong in sixteen ways.

I can choose no cups right and four cups wrong in one way.

And the correct result: four cups right and none wrong—one way.

Out of seventy ways of choosing there is only one way to choose the correct result. I am certainly *feeling* less confident, although I know how I *feel* won't influence the actual results.

6. THE NULL HYPOTHESIS

To each there is an opposite. Every experiment may be said to exist only in order to give the facts a chance of proving the opposite—the null hypothesis. If the results show I am unable to discriminate between the cups of tea on the basis of which ingredient was added first—milk or tea—then the null hypothesis is true.

If a woman who claimed she was good consistently acts as if she is bad to the point beyond that of statistical error, the null hypothesis is proved—she is bad.

7. RANDOMIZATION

As the subject of the experiment I could insist that all of the cups of tea be exactly alike—same thickness and smoothness of cups, same temperature, strength, and exact amounts of tea and milk. With labor and expense these lurking variables could be removed but Robert says they do not, in fact, constitute significant refinements to the experiment. It is his view that it is an essential characteristic of experimentation that it is carried out with limited resources.

"Whatever level of care and skill is expended on improving and equalizing conditions, they will always be to a greater or lesser extent unsatisfactory. The *experimenter* chooses which causes of disturbance should be acted on and which should be ignored."

8. RECORDING

Robert has ruled up a page in his notebook for the results. He shows me where to write out the hypothesis and the experimental method. There's not much to it, sort of like a baking recipe but strangely back to front. Instead of adding things together and getting something for it at the end, you start with an idea and then take things away.

Robert has two notebooks—"Field," for notes taken in the soil and cropping wagon and the various paddocks where we stop, and "Laboratory." As the train has no laboratory he uses this book for notes taken while leaning on a dinner tray on top of his bunk. He has chosen the field notebook for the results of the tea experiment—my experiment—and for some reason I feel disappointed by that.

9. RESULTS

The actual experiment—the drinking and classification of the tea—is postponed as we are due at Rainbow shortly and the agriculture men have called a meeting to consolidate, as Robert puts it, "the plan of attack." I wash all the cups and pack the equipment away—kettle, tea, water, milk, teaspoons, and napkins.

Robert says science never loses its moment, and that we will have plenty of opportunity to complete the experiment at a later date.

There was another incident between Jeparit and Rainbow. It was a day of traveling when we seemed to be pushing through the wheat, inching along as if caught in the doldrums on a mealy yellow sea. Mr. Ohno flew a tiny paper crane into my lap as I sat sewing in the sitting car. Under one wing it said, *Has teas?* When I looked up he was gone.

I told Mary I was going for thread and then I followed him back down the train to the poultry car. Mr. Ohno's bunk was behind the cages—a cot roped off with a patterned curtain. I could see him crouched behind it and coughed quietly so he would know I was there. He stood up and held the curtain back for me, bowing so low, in such a small space, I thought his head would touch my stomach.

"Some tea?"

He had placed two cushions on the floor next to the cot. In between them a tiny green porcelain teapot sat on a wire grill with a lit candle flickering beneath it. He handed me a small bowl and motioned at the cushion.

"Sit, Miss Jean."

I watched as he lowered himself on his haunches in one swift movement, as if hinged at the hips and knees. He looked away politely as I wrapped my dress around my legs and made an ungainly descent to the cushion. I went to speak—to ask about the brand of tea and the cups without handles—but he looked up at me sharply and placed his finger in front of his lips. So I sat and watched him make the tea, which, despite the rocking of the train, he did with great precision. I noticed the angles at which he placed the pot and the bowls and the serious, languid way he lifted the tea to his lips. I copied his use of both hands around the warm bowl and when I lifted them in front of me, it felt something like praying.

It was very quiet in the poultry car—just the sound of the train coursing over the rails and the gentle scratching and cheeping of the chickens. Mr. Ohno's clothes hung like apparitions above his cot and against the curtain so I had the impression I was in his company several times over. The crouching was becoming uncomfortable as my dress was strained tightly across my outer thighs. Looser garments would be required to sit like this for any length of time. I rubbed my hands over the taut material and considered asking Mr. Ohno the Japanese word for thigh. I suspected his language was more exact and would have separate words for the two different regions—outer thigh and inner thigh.

I had just drained my bowl when the train rounded a bend and we both leaned sideways into the curve. My elbow raised the sheet on Mr. Ohno's cot and I saw underneath it several piles of what looked like tiny pieces of mattress stacked on top of one another. I sneaked another look. Sandwiches. Mr. Ohno's luncheon sandwiches were stacked neatly under his bed in a repeating pattern of bread, jam, bread, honey, bread, vegemite, bread . . . They were completely dried out and didn't smell at all. I smoothed back the sheet and pretended that I hadn't seen.

7

WELCOME TO WYCHEPROOF

I wrap the veil in brown paper and leave it in Mary's pigeonhole. She rarely checks for circulars so it will be weeks before she finds it.

I tell Mary that my marriage to Robert will be about *more* than love. It will be a modern marriage, in which Robert and I, as free and independent units of production, will implement the proven facts of scientific research. In which we will take the miniaturized world of the train and live it large, at real-life scale. Robert will grow his superior superphosphated wheats and, once the wheat has been milled, I will document his success by baking the annual test loaves in my experimental kitchen.

"Is this you speaking or him speaking, Jeanie?"

"It's a partnership. The one can't work without the other. It's a marriage and a special sort of partnership. You can't say he hasn't got purpose."

"No. I can't," Mary said dryly.

"And we will be together—and have some land around us. I was thinking I could plant some fruit trees. Start a bit of an orchard?"

Mary was silent for a minute, then she reached out and took my hand. "You mustn't agree just because he asked you. Others will ask you. You may not believe it now, but they will."

The train will stop at Wycheproof just long enough for Robert and me to disembark. It is heading for a two-day demonstration in Sea Lake and then on to Swan Hill. After that it will leave the Mallee and follow the Murray River to the orchard country around Echuca.

It isn't a bad time to be leaving. The superintendent has hinted that this may be the last tour—the agriculture minister is concerned about expenditure in these "difficult times." Robert has organized our leaving in great detail. The local priest will conduct the ceremony—he has a sister who will witness for us—then our new neighbor, a Mr. Ivers, will drive us out to the farm. The Wycheproof general store has filled Robert's telegraphed order, and all of our linen, crockery, kitchenware, and domestic staples will be ready for collection. We will do all of this in one day— leave the train, get married, collect our belongings, and travel to our new home. It will be the first full day that we have spent together.

Mallee mornings don't flicker. There are no hazy beginnings, no half-light of hesitation where day meets night. The Mallee sun snaps over the horizon with the sure and sudden glow of electric light. Long, sharp rays of yellow reach across the flat horizon like tentacles. I have seen this before. On a packet of Mildura raisins. *Raisins, Full of Goodness from the Sun. Eat More Raisins Every Day in Every Way.* The picture on the packet shows children frolicking in a paddock of golden wheat wearing neat shorts and knitted jumpers; the sun's rays touch them like ribbons from a maypole.

The blinds in our sleeping compartment lift methodically with every jolt of the train to let in a pulse of light. The inside of my mouth is dry from sleep. Mary snores a little above me. She has hung my wedding costume on the back of the compartment door and I watch it dancing to the movement of the train. I have made myself a suit in dove gray wool with a double-lapel jacket in the French style. The lapels sit high on my chest and curve upward like the wings of a bird. There is a buttonhole that I would like to fill with a gardenia, although I imagine such a thing may be hard to come by in Wycheproof.

Mary stirs above me.

"I have a present for you, Jean. But you can't have it until we stop." Her voice is a little high and strained. She climbs down from her bunk to braid my hair, her eyes swimming. She winds the braids into two scrolls over each ear and pins them securely. She says these snail shells suit me better than a bun. At twenty-three I already have some gray hairs threaded through the brown. We dress and pack, both glad to be caught up in the detail of something.

My bags overflow with presents—a set of notes from Sister Crock on domestic science and modern housewifery ("*Every-thing* you'll need to know is in here"). A Fowler's Bottling Outfit from Mr. Baker (the recipe for jellied pig's trotters has been underlined). Mr. Plattfuss has made me a model of the train in tin with pipe-cleaner animals peeping from the wagons. It looks like a child's toy, except, as he points out to me, for the handy bottle opener welded onto the underside. A surprising set of postcards from Mr. Ohno, and a pair of gloves from Mr. Talbot. The gloves are a fleshy pink and I know whenever I wear them I will be reminded of the tissue diseases of sheep.

I sit shoulder to shoulder with Mary amongst the gifts and gaze out the window. Mary has decided that we must stay in the sleeping compartment to avoid the bad luck of seeing Robert too soon before the ceremony.

The train rolls quietly through the Mallee. There are two ways to look at the wheat. I am used to taking in a great expanse, seeing a whole paddock from fence to fence. A paddock of uniform height and color held in by silvery wires. Or you can see it in close-up. Pick out an individual stem, follow it to its wispy beard, and then let your eye flow over the sea of soft interwoven heads like a mat suspended above the ground.

It is only when you see the wheat this second way that you notice how it moves. I had thought of it as a sea, pushed about by the wind like a tide. But it is not at all like that. When you watch it close up, a field of wheat is full of whirls and dips and eddies that can slow in an instant to complete stillness. There is no logic to it. A small patch in the center of a paddock can be thrashing while the rest moves in a slow and lazy wave.

I think it must be necessary, when you live in it, to start seeing the wheat in this close-up way. There is no point in focusing on the horizon, on what lies beyond what the eye can see; the truth of the matter is right here.

I can feel the sweat spreading out from my spine. It is fine and hot like yesterday, like the day before. Wycheproof is in the southern Mallee, on the border of the Wimmera. It lies in the center of a shallow basin of flat country fringed with low hills. The train tracks slice through the center of the basin, dividing the land on either side. It is the only town in Victoria where the train runs along the main street. As we mount the ridge of the hill, two huge wheat silos come into view; all the buildings around them look squat in comparison. Mary has her head out the window as we approach the station.

"It's a lovely big station—with a rose garden."

The train doesn't slow. We are coming in too fast. I'm anxious and perhaps a little relieved that it mightn't stop. We pass the station at a stately pace. It is deserted except for a hot old collie stretched under the shade of the veranda. The train veers sharply to the left and straightens into the main street.

Mary is excited: "They're going to stop here for you. Right in the center of town!"

The main street is enormously wide. There is a road on both sides of the railway line edged with a row of shops. The train jerks and hisses to a stop opposite the post office, which is large and topped by an old-fashioned clock.

We run across the carriage from window to window, unsure which side to get out. I look up and down the train on both sides for Robert but I can't see him. He must be slow about his good-byes. Finally Mary tugs the right side door open, jumps down, and turns to help me.

"Quick. I have something for you. Don't worry about your bags, the guard will get them."

I want to tell Mary to slow down. I don't want to leave like this—it feels too sudden. I'm not sure anymore if I want to leave at all, but Mary is dragging me by the hand along the side of the train and we are running through a cloud of steam. The steam has settled on my face or maybe I am crying. We are in front of the cattle trucks. The train is hugely tall without a station platform in front of it. Mary calls through the slats to a stock hand

and a ramp crashes down. Before the dust has settled the youngest stock hand leads out a cow. Not any cow, _our_ cow— the folly cow. She shifts her weight from leg to leg, blinking in the dust and light and steam.

Mary takes her halter from the stock hand and gives it to me. She is grinning from ear to ear. "For you, Jean. I arranged it all with Mr. Plattfuss. She'll be better off with you. She would just have ended up in a paddock somewhere. She can remind you of me. And she'll be, you know, something to love. . . ."

I hold Mary tight. The ramp is pulled up and the train sounds a deep chuff—it is about to leave. Folly's halter is stiff in my hand. It is new; Mary has plaited it from baling twine. She pulls away from me and runs back to our compartment, blowing me kisses over her shoulder.

"Write," she calls out. "Write to me with all of your results!"

The door slams. I step back and look up into the windows of the train. The men wave at me from the windows of the dairy car. Mr. Baker whistles through his orange whiskers. Mr. Plattfuss wags a mocking finger at Folly; the startling silk of Mr. Ohno's tie concertinas as he bows. Then a jolt and they all tumble sideways into one another as the train lurches off.

A rumble of steam, and the final carriage glides past. It slips away like a curtain and reveals the other side of the street, where Robert is standing with his bags and cases. He is wearing a blue suit I have never seen before and squinting into the sun.

The folly cow won't budge. She watches the rear of the train snaking off up the street and lets out a long wet moo. Robert strides across the tracks. There is the sound of fly screen doors banging shut as people go back about their business.

"You got out of the other side."

"Yes. I got out of the other side."

He reaches for Folly's halter. "You should have told me about the cow, Jean. What am I going to do with an old scrub cow?"

"She's not for you. She's for me—from Mary."

Robert's face is red. Droplets of sweat glisten in his eyebrows. The suit must be hot.

Robert ties Folly to a fence behind the hardware store and carries our bags inside. I wait for him on the veranda—trying to breathe slowly and drain the heat that has risen to my face. My gray suit feels too tight and too showy. Women come and go from shop to shop, many tailed by little children. A group has gathered in front of the pharmacy several doors down. The women make a loose circle of nodding heads. They laugh loudly. I look away. A small child tumbles from the footpath onto the street. The women gather around him cooing and scolding.

The church is on a side street and the ceremony is quick. The priest's collar is too tight and he switches the Bible from hand to hand as he tugs at it. He aims his words into the hot air above our heads; I feel almost as if I can see them, coasting over the empty pews and floating down to the floor. Robert takes my hand—for the ring—but the priest pulls him up.

"Don't bother, Mr. Pettergree, on a day like today she'll have fingers like sausages. Do it later, when it cools down."

Stan Hercules is waiting outside to take our photograph for the *Wycheproof Ensign*. And then Muriel, the priest's sister, is saying welcome to Wycheproof, Mrs. Pettergree, and telling me about the dramatic society and the CWA and the Younger Set and tennis and how she won the ladies' nail-driving competition at the Berriwillock Floral Ball until, finally, I am sitting in the backseat of Mr. Ivers's car, looking at my husband's neck, so red, in front of me.

"I expect we'll see you in town soon, Mrs. Pettergree," Muriel shouts through the window, but she has to jump back quickly as we are off; Mr. Ivers is keen to get away.

Our farm is on the Avoca River and Mr. Ivers is our closest neighbor. He has maintained the land since the last farmer and his family walked off with only their suitcases and tickets on a ship to New Zealand—"regular rain, proper English soils." I wonder what Mr. Ivers thinks about the farm being taken up by a scientist and agricultural expert rather than an ordinary farmer.

The car has been sitting in the sun and I feel like I am being baked alive but the men don't remove their coats. Robert quizzes Ivers about local yields. We skirt around the tiny mountain and take the Boort Road out through the paddocks. A few miles on we branch off down a narrower track and Ivers turns and smiles at me shyly.

"This is it, then," he says.

I smile back, dabbing at the sweat on my cheeks. At the start of a long driveway gum trees stand in a clump like monuments. Robert gets out to open the gate. The trunk of the nearest tree is as thick as the bodies of several men. At head height it splits into three separate prongs. Its delicate purple bark hangs in strips, a golden flesh shining underneath.

"How old are these trees?" I ask Mr. Ivers.

"Not sure, missus. A hundred, maybe two hundred."

As the car pulls away I imagine us inching up the paper on Robert's hand-drawn map. Inching towards the *J* for Jean. Robert reaches back and touches my arm when we pull up in front of the house as if to counteract any disappointment I might be feeling. But I like the plainness of the house. It is not unlike the cottage in the orchard—solidly square with two small windows each side of the door. The paint has faded from white to oily gray.

Ivers says that his wife, Elsie, has cleaned and aired for us and that he has moved most of the furniture back from where it was stored in the shed. He says there is even an old piano.

I imagine myself describing the house in a letter to my aunt—although we no longer write: *I have left my position on the Better-Farming Train to marry an English Scientist. We have a farm in the Mallee with a small cottage.* I would need to say something about a cat. In letters to my aunt I always included a reference to cats. *I have recently rescued a stray cat, been feeding a cat for a friend, had to borrow a cat for mousing, was kept awake by a cat, or saw an especially large or beautifully patterned cat in my travels.*

Robert steps up onto the veranda, opens the front door, and disappears inside. His boots reverberate on the floorboards. Ivers is leaning against the car, half looking at me. He has taken off his coat and I can see he is a careful man—belt and braces. I'm not ready to go into the house, although I know this is what I'm expected to do—to follow Robert. Instead I walk under an old peppercorn and along the side path to the backyard—bare dirt with a few mulgas. The house has a sloping broom-brush veranda that dips low over the back door like a messy fringe. A slack wire fence holds in the wheat.

I am struck by the quietness. For the past year I have been

surrounded by the noises of the train: birds, animals, men, machines. Now there is just the company of plants. I understand a little why the wheat men who visited the train were so stunned by the colorful cacophony of it.

I walk over to the fence that holds the wheat in. I look back at the house and then at the wheat again. The wheat looks smooth, almost like water. It is "in boot"—just up to my thighs. I am unbearably hot and I feel like it might be cooler amongst the wheat. I part the wires and step through the fence. The first few steps are satisfying. I feel like I'm getting somewhere and there is the sound of the wheat snapping and the warm, mealy smell of it. But I haven't gone far when the stems start to bunch around my legs. Shards pierce my stockings. My suit is oddly twisted around me. The horizon seesaws sharply in the distance. I am falling. The wheat crackles around me. I call out weakly in the direction of the house. A flash of check shirt hurries along the side path. Then Mr. Ivers ducks between the wires. He lifts me easily and carries me back to the house, curling his boot around the front door to open it. Robert is in the hallway, carrying a box of pots and pans.

Ivers laughs good-naturedly. "Heatstroke. Your missus was in a spot of bother, Pettergree. Oh, and I'm afraid I've just carried her over the threshold."

Robert smiles weakly and nods towards the bedroom, where I am put to rest on the dusty mattress.

I sleep a little while Robert unpacks and sees to the delivery of Folly. Later, over a cold supper, he says there are no suitable paddocks for her and he expects she will be stupid enough to trample the crops. Stupid enough is plainly meant for me.

"I was just going for a walk. I thought I'd walk along the creek, only I couldn't find it for the wheat."

Robert opens his notebook. His hands shake slightly as he jots down some figures. "This isn't a demonstration plot or a wagonload, Jean—this is the real thing."

I find my walk. I find the narrow river. It is little more than a creek. I lead Folly there each day after Robert leaves the house and sit and sew on the steep banks. Folly is restless. She likes my sewing basket and clumps down to push it about with her big flat face. I am embroidering a handkerchief for Mary—Folly in the wheat. I have only an egg yolk yellow so the wheat looks wrong, but it would be impossible to capture the true, russety hue of it in thread.

Sometimes I walk down the driveway back to the thick sugar gum at the gate. The ledge in between the three prongs holds me snugly. Ant trails curve around the trunks. If I look up for long enough I can see where the ends of the very farthest branches spike the sky.

Bill Ivers's wife, Elsie, is a broad-shouldered woman with a large face in two parts. The under-hat area of her forehead is very white and smooth, while the skin below it is red and boiled-looking from the sun. Elsie has made several visits bringing cakes and eggs. She leads the children over on an old Clydesdale. All boys, they increase evenly in size and age between withers and rump. Off the horse they are attracted to one another like magnets, tumbling and wrestling in a constant whirl of activity that turns their small faces steaming pink.

On her first visit she arrives with a fruitcake, carrying it on a plate while leading the horse. I make tea while she sniffs suspiciously around the kitchen and snorts at the wheat heads Robert has pinned out for dissection on the table.

"I wouldn't be letting my husband bring dirty muck like that inside."

"It's science, Mrs. Ivers. It's important work."

"Still dirty, though, ain't it? And you'd better be calling me Elsie."

We take two kitchen chairs out under the broom brush and watch the boys fight one another with mulga branches.

"They're a trial, Jean, both men and boys, but I'm sure you'll find that out soon enough." She looks at me side on, at the space I take up in my dress.

Elsie's mother minds the boys the first time she takes me into town. Elsie wears her best dress, a white number with broad pink and orange stripes, a bit like a winter sheet. She drives very slowly with her hat pulled low over her brow. We have only just turned onto the main road when the car narrowly misses a brown snake surfing, head up, for the shade of the roadside gums.

I would have liked to explore the town alone but Elsie ushers me from shop to shop. My gaze is drawn to the train tracks in front of the post office and I am tempted to find the place I first got down and stand awhile, but Elsie would think it odd.

There is everything in Wycheproof that you could need: several banks, the handsome post office fit for a city square, a greengrocer's, a butcher, a pharmacy and haberdashery, a newsagent, garages, and two general stores. With the train tracks in the center and the wide, dark verandas, it is not possible to see people on one side of the street from the other. Many of the businesses are replicated, sometimes in exactly the same position on each side. Elsie crossed the street with me so we could at least walk past all the shops, but she told me that many people in the town shopped on only one side depending on the hotel of their menfolk—Commercial or Terminus.

At my request we visit the free library in the Mechanics' Institute. It is only a few shelves in a curtained-off corner behind the pool table but there is a full-time librarian—Miss Iris Pfundt. Miss Pfundt is well turned out but there is something dried up and scratchy about her. Her powder blue skirt suit sits stiffly on her sharp frame and she smells of stale hair spray. She gives me a membership card and shows me the five different categories of books: detective, light love, Wild West, children's, and heavy. Heavy is Adam Smith's *The Wealth of Nations* and Froude's *History of England*. I ask if there is any science. Miss Pfundt shakes her head without moving her tight yellow curls, and snorts.

"I hope you're not going to be like the high school girls—hard to please with all those modern plays and poetry. I'm very particular. We only have *nice* books here. I throw away anything dirty."

The membership card requires Robert's signature so I tell her I'll be back.

Last call is the butcher. The woman in front of us at the counter asks for the cheap mince and slowly counts out her pennies. She is flanked by a large daughter who stares glumly at her scuffed tennis shoes.

The butcher works behind a green fly-wire screen and hands the packages through a flap. He passes the mince through to the young woman. "Cheer up, Olive, it's not the end of the world." He winks at her mother. "Boy troubles, no doubt."

Elsie pushes to the front and leans in close to the screen to place her order.

The butcher smiles at her playfully, tosses his tongs in the air, and snaps them together as he catches them. "The best cuts for the lovely Mrs. Ivers," he calls teasingly to an apprentice in the back room.

I pretend to read the chalkboard, which lists the prices and has the butchery slogan: *Hommelfhof Brothers' Family Butchers— Where Honest Dealing Creates Good Feeling.* Good feeling indeed. Elsie smooths her stripey dress around her hips and opens her dusty purse.

"Wasted on the farm, you are, Mrs. Ivers. We should see you in town more often. And your new little neighbor too," he says, cutting me a glance.

8

THE EXPERIMENTAL KITCHEN

Sister Crock wasn't wholly against men. "In kitchen design," she said, "they have their uses. Being apt to come up with good ideas about using wheels, inclined planes, pivoting storage walls, pulleys, and electric light."

She didn't want me to leave the train. It meant getting another girl from the Emily McPherson College of Domestic Science, sifting through the marriage fodder until she found someone with a calling.

"How can you leave?" she said. "How can you go somewhere so flat? You deserve better."

Sister Crock thought flatness meant dullness. She was wrong. It isn't dull and it isn't even flat. Not in winter. All summer the wheat makes a false horizon; it camouflages the real angle of the land. But in winter it isn't flat at all. It swerves and undulates for miles. There are sharp rises in the middle of paddocks, hills around fence posts, steep mounds edging dams.

And I have my calling. I can't spell it out. I can't say *exactly* what it is that I want, but I know what I don't want. I don't want

73

to teach something I haven't lived. I don't want to be always with women. I don't want evenings in the common room playing bridge and crazy euchre. I don't want to be like Sister Crock, spectating and directing life from the outer—I want a chance to feel it and taste it for myself.

From the kitchen I can see Robert working the ground with the cultivator. He's experimenting with the stubble—working out how long to leave it between each treatment. Every time he goes over the same piece of ground it's called a pass. It makes me think of flying. That he's just passing over the place—taking a look, storing up the picture in his mind like someone out sightseeing.

For the first month Robert left the house every day just after dawn. He measured and recorded all the farm's soils and crops. At lunchtime he brought in wheat samples that were either remarkably good or remarkably bad. He spread them out on the kitchen table and drew sketches of them in his notebook. I found the sample plants unnerving—most of them are thin and feeble-stalked with flailing arms like the skeletons of children. The sampling and recording continued for several weeks until the kitchen floor was covered with plants pinned to sheets of newspaper and stacked loosely in groups: Rust Evident; Excessively Short Straw; Weak Tillering; Poor Stem Extension at Peeping; Immature Head. It was difficult for me to start my own work with the kitchen so full and the dead plants high around my ankles.

When at last they were cleared away I set up the experimental kitchen—checking the timers, temperature gauges, scales, and measuring apparatus. Everything must be rigidly standard-

ized. When I pull the test loaves from the oven for the final as-
sessment of crumb structure, crust color, and loaf volume, the
only variable must be Robert's flour. My involvement must be
rendered invisible by the strict adherence to procedure. It is an
enormous responsibility. All of Robert's paddock science will
come together in this kitchen in ten test loaves a year.

But after lunch each day, when I sit facing Robert at the
kitchen table, instead of familiarizing myself with the electric
proving cabinet, something else happens. I can't describe how it
starts—maybe our breathing lengthens or shortens slightly so it
falls together? Or maybe one of us might move a little so that
the angles of our bodies are somehow shifted? I might be looking
out the window, showing the side of my neck, some collarbone,
when he places his hand heavily on my shoulder. The feeling,
when it rises, is so intense, the need for each other so urgent,
nothing is fast enough. The table is pushed out of the way,
clothes shed, sometimes ripped, bodies held with force. Then we
are coupling hurriedly wherever we might fall. In front of the
pantry, against the sink, even on the table, my hair in a puddle
of lukewarm tea. On days when Robert is clearly tired from carting water and we have barely even talked, I always think it
might not happen, but it is enough for me just to brush my hand
against his wrist as I remove his plate. Then he stands abruptly
and grips my waist. His Adam's apple bobs as he swallows hard. I
am still standing, still holding the plate, when he pushes my
dress aside and takes my nipple into his mouth.

Odd thoughts break through during the lovemaking. I think
it is because of the kitchen. A small part of my mind can't seem
to let go of the fact that we are in the kitchen. One day as we

are coupled in front of the oven, moving rhythmically, sinuously together, I am suddenly back in elementary housewifery with Mrs. Vera Cornthwaite introducing a lesson on the removal of loose dirt.

"What about fixed dirt, Mrs. Cornthwaite?" a girl asked enthusiastically from the back of the class.

"One must learn to crawl before one can walk, dear," Mrs. Cornthwaite replied. "Fixed dirt is covered in advanced housewifery. You'll have to wait until second year."

Another time when we are joined side by side, my head jammed underneath his chin, his hand gripping my buttocks, drawing out their rise and fall, I notice the sharp red-white divide of his forearm where he folds his shirtsleeve. In the sun, out of the sun. In. Out. And I'm thinking of a lecture on homemaking and how to welcome a guest.

"Even if you have little space—no actual guest room—have a folding canvas cot ready for guests. Make a space for your guest's things in the same place. He won't feel comfortable using a few drawers in one room, a wardrobe in another, a mirror in a third. Make sure you can quickly and easily set up the bed. If you aren't sure you can do it fast, have a cot drill once in a while."

Perhaps it was drill. The word *drill*.

Sometimes Robert cries during our afternoons of sex and I feel very tenderly for him. I think of the little girl Sister Crock brought in as a test pupil for teaching practice. She was only nine or ten, in a stiff gray pinafore with sallow skin and yellowing hair. She sat on a chair at the front of the room facing the audience while Sister Crock lectured from behind her.

"Teaching domestic science provides an especially rich opportunity for the moral training of the child. As the subject is active the 'real child' is more likely to be manifested than when she sits quietly at her desk. By the very nature of the work, the child is constantly confronted with the results of such delinquencies as dishonesty, selfishness, shirking, and slackness. An honestly made pudding will speak for itself, as will one that has been the victim of the greedy child who, thinking to gain personal advantage, has helped herself to extra butter or shortening and spoiled her produce."

The little girl blinked and a tear wobbled slowly down her cheek. But she held her head high. Challenging us. Was she the good pudding or the bad? I wanted to leave my seat and go and hold her. And to scold Sister Crock for using the child so unfairly.

But back to Robert. The odd thoughts go in both directions. When lovemaking I often think about homemaking and vice versa. One morning as I plot a time-and-motion study of the kitchen—I am considering moving the mixing center to make it more efficient—I am suddenly thinking of Robert's naked, rutting back. How his tailbone dips and moves at such an angle his back looks double-jointed. Surely it must be free from the rest of his spine to thrust with such force? Then I'm thinking of my second year of the diploma when we made string studies of movement patterns around the college kitchens. One girl washed up or made a meal while another followed her movements on a pegboard, winding a ball of string from one place to another. The string picture showed how often she retraced her steps, how much energy she used. The aim was motion-mindedness—

becoming aware of your repetitive, unnecessary, or superfluous movements. There was a special unit of work on it in third year.

> *Choose two subjects from:*
> *Making thrifty contrivances*
> *Rich cake mixtures*
> *Basic infant care*
> *Simple butchery*
> *Household mending*
> *Motion-mindedness*

This is how I think of these early afternoons in the kitchen with Robert—that they are filled with a particular sort of motion-mindedness. We have slipped through the science to a place of pure and perfect motion.

RESULTS FROM THE 1935 HARVEST

The sample has a low bushel weight (61 lbs). In accordance with standard sampling procedure a portion of FAQ (fair–average quality) wheat was critically examined and subjected to analysis and a milling test in the experimental flour mill.

The sample is very bright and plump, and has a generally pleasing appearance. The moisture content and the protein content are normal.

Purpose: To measure the quality of wheats grown by Mr. R. L. Pettergree of Wycheproof in regard to high yields of good-colored flour with superior baking quality.

Comments: At this stage not all of the wheat milled for flour for these tests has been grown under the experimental regime (some of it being grown by the previous farmer).

Quality Tests: The Pelshenke figure, which indicates gluten quality (time taken for dough ball to expand under water at temperature; time divided by protein content = quality), is average. Mechanical testing of the physical properties of the dough using Brabender's Farinograph and Fermentograph shows average flour quality with acceptable gas-producing power.

LOAF NO.	CRUMB STRUCTURE	CRUST COLOR	LOAF VOLUME	TOTAL
1	8/10	7/10	7/10	22/30
2	6/10	7/10	8/10	21/30
3	7/10	7/10	7/10	21/30
4	7/10	6/10	7/10	20/30
5	8/10	8/10	7/10	23/30
6	6/10	7/10	8/10	21/30
7	4/10	7/10	5/10	16/30
8	8/10	8/10	7/10	23/30
9	8/10	6/10	9/10	23/30
10	7/10	8/10	7/10	22/30

It takes three days. The loaves are large and well formed, except for number seven, which I rushed and may not have measured properly. I am making sketches of their shapes.

I expect noticeably better results next year, when Robert's regime is fully in place. I pin the results above the oven, then I take some of the test loaves over to Elsie next door. She sniffs at them suspiciously but says thank you all the same.

9

MR. OHNO'S GIFT

"Is this who you are? Are you someone who looks at these things? Are you someone who does this?" He holds the postcards out to me, red velvet spilling through his fingers. My hands fly to my face.

"Well?"

"I didn't buy them, Robert. I didn't ask for them. They were a gift—from Mr. Ohno."

"A tasty gift, Jean. A tasty gift for *my* wife." A line of stringy spittle bounces elastic from his lower lip. He pushes my hands down.

"No. Please. I'm sorry. It's not what you think."

"So what is it, then? What do you call this, then?" He throws the postcards onto the table and jabs at them with his forefinger, separating them, spreading them out. A crooked jumble of fleshy shadows—breasts and thighs and in most of them the dark rectangular outline of a car.

"Do you admire the vehicles, Jean? Are you a student of the motorcar?"

81

"No."

He picks up one of the cards and holds it in front of my face. "Here, Jean. Tell me what you see."

"Please. I can't."

The postcard falls to the floor and lands between my feet.

"Pick it up, woman. Pick it up."

I crouch down slowly and want to stay there—to not have to get up again.

"Stand up, Jean. Come on, stand up. Tell me what you see."

"Don't, please. It's humiliating."

He snorts and thrusts his hands into his pockets.

"Two women in a car."

"More precise, I think, Jean. More exact. Be a bit more systematic about it. That's what I've taught you, haven't I? What sort of car?"

"A Ford."

"Two women in a Ford. Are they going shopping? Going to the pictures?"

"They're . . . they're . . . touching each other."

Robert brings his fingers to his temples as if to divert a strong current passing through his brain. I look at the postcard again. Two women, both with such ordinary faces—lipstick, neat permanents. One has a slightly hooked nose and the other is a little jowly. Although they wear no clothes they have a "dressed" look, as if they have rushed out in a hurry.

Both of them wear necklaces and earrings and dark leather watchbands. One holds her handbag coyly in front of her sex. They are not young women. They have round arms and thighs and soft bellies. The woman in the foreground holds one of her breasts, her fingers splayed scissorlike around the square nub of nipple. Her other hand is on the thigh of her friend. I can see where the flesh dimples from the pressure of the upholstery.

Robert snatches the postcard from my hand and crushes it. He sobs. Tears catch in the deep grooves around his open mouth. His lips are stretched tight around his teeth.

"I'll throw them away. I'm sorry. They were a wedding gift. I don't really know why he gave them to me and I didn't mean to keep them."

Mr. Ohno had cornered me in the domestic hygiene car one afternoon as I was refilling the Insectibane atomizers. I heard his clogs on the wooden floor behind me and turned to find the top of his head a few inches from my thighs. The bow. Mr. Ohno's bow was always close enough and long enough for an inspection of the childlike shape of his head and the immaculate line of his part.

He straightened, took the atomizer from my hand, and held it teasingly like a gun at his head.

"I shoot mysel for you, Miss Jean?"

"It's too late, Mr. Ohno, I'm taken."

He shook his head and made a sad clucking noise.

"Miss Jean, you like the country Af-ri-ca. You big, dark." He cleared his throat in preparation for a difficult word: "Mysterious." He beamed with achievement.

An embarrassed flush crept up my neck. "Sturdy. People generally say I'm sturdy, Mr. Ohno. And Africa's not a country. It's a continent."

"Ah, Miss Jean." Mr. Ohno waggled his head again. He was

not interested in geography. Or in retrospect perhaps he was—
in the hills and valleys of the female body.

"I have p'esent for you." He produced a square of red velvet
from the breast pocket of his coat. It looked like a small book
and I started to unfold the cloth when he placed his hands
firmly over mine.

"No. Not now, Miss Jean, open later when by you alone.".

The tendons dance in Robert's forearms as he reaches out to
me. I gather him in. I can feel the roots of his arms working deep
within his back. I am reminded of Sister Crock's nursing man-
ual, an illustration of "The Musculature of the Human Male"—
a mass of sinuous pink fibers, of strong ropes knotting and
interweaving.

"Jean." His voice is thick with feeling.

Sex to make good is not like ordinary sex. Each tiny movement, a reaching lip, the long blink of an eye, is imbued with a
slow and heavy meaning. We peel away our clothes. There is no
embarrassed fumble, he hangs above me tensely, dipping and
straining.

Afterwards, with his body half across me, his face in my hair,
he whispers, "You're not a, a . . . tabby, are you?"

"Oh, Robert, of course not."

He makes me tea and we move from the floor to the bed,
where he tells me the story of Lillian and wets my slip with his
tears.

10

LILLIAN'S TASTE FOR SOIL

1905

Robert was the firstborn. Little Enid came next. Little Enid born with the cavity in her back—a crater of pink and scarlet tissue and the glinting white gristle of her backbone.

"You could put a potato in it, couldn't you, Robbie?" said his mother, Lillian.

He was worried that she would—worried at the waste of a good potato. The wound shone and leaked and sucked at the special rags it was covered with.

Two weeks later Robbie was up on the moors fetching a bunch for the coffin. No cut flowers for Enid. Robbie wrenched a branch of gorse and came home with yellow flowers in his hair. It was something to look at during the dismal service in the parlor—the torn branch of the gorse all stringy where he had wrenched it around and around. Three men carried the coffin away, each with a Woodbine between his lips. Three orange dots glowed in the dark when they stumbled back later arguing about who would go upstairs and give our Lillian some comfort.

She's always out, our Lillian, and she hardly ever cooks for him. Food comes from the pocket of her lilac coat with the foxy collar—tinned meat, soda bread, potatoes, a handful of tea threaded with lint. When she has a man Robbie waits downstairs. He dreams the parlor chair is alive—a smooth chestnut pony galloping over the moors—and wakes to find his leg caught in a bulge of greasy horsehair.

"Red hair," say the men who meet him on the stairs as he goes up to take their place. Sometimes they light a match and search for something in his face as it flares. "Jesus, you're like your mother, boy, red hair and bones like sticks."

Lillian's hair is red as holly berries, red as Christmas, red as the tin of Carnation milk she shares with Robbie. The skin on her face is spread with large mustard freckles but her private skin— breasts, bunchy stomach, round thighs—is see-through white.

Robbie wakes each winter's night panicking and congested. He struggles to dislodge the blankets, coats, and newspapers that cover him. He reaches for Lillian or bangs on the wall to rouse her. The air is as cold as water against his face. He sucks, trying to separate something dry and breathable from the wet. He sucks more and more; in a long, continual hiss, his chest and belly blowing up and up—a trap of air. He imagines his insides creaky and dry like a pair of kitchen bellows except at the very tip there is a hole, a wound that he must fill, or try to fill with air. The nights are long with sucking and heaving and with Lillian trickling tonic over his dry lips. In the morning they lie tumbled together in exhaustion.

Nanna Pett supplies Robbie's tonic. It comes bottled and then boxed with a poster of the Olympic Games marathon route showing all the sights from Windsor to White City. Burly men run high-kneed along the route, wearing what look to Robbie like their underclothes. They swig from bottles of Owbridge's Lung Tonic and sternly advise: *Don't buy cheap imitations.* No one runs in Yorkshire. Robbie has seen the millworkers on the common playing nipsey. He's watched them, stripped to vests and braces, swing the knur, follow the fly of the spell, and argue about bets. They huddle and saunter and swing the club, but nobody is actually going anywhere.

Robbie notices, on a long night of wakefulness, that Lillian has trouble of her own. She is up again and again squatting over the chipped potty at the end of the bed. He watches out of half-closed eyes and sees that she is full with piss, her belly is as tight as a tank.

Nanna Pett brings bread and candles, the bottom bits of rice pudding, and stale parkin wrapped in greaseproof paper. She starts to come more and more often and the men all but disappear. Lillian is always home now and always hungry. Robbie catches her chipping flakes of kalsomine from the walls and melting them on her tongue like holy wafers. She sucks coal dirt from under her fingernails, chews at the sleeve of her lilac coat. She takes the tonic spoon and sits on the back step digging at the soil and answers Robbie's questioning squint with a word.

"Brown—it tastes brown."

They share. They always share. Except for Robbie's treasures hidden in a tin box underneath the bed—a postcard of Louis Blériot crossing the Channel in his bright orange airplane, a label from a Bovril jar of a smiling man in driving hat and goggles, and the Olympic Games marathon poster. Robbie's treasures are about adventures—going somewhere else, running, driving, flying, getting away.

Then Robbie is sent away. Nanna Pett comes to get him on her bicycle for Lillian's confinement. He pulls his spare socks from the line and fills his pockets with soil from the yard. He is taken to Auntie Flo's in town. Flo is Lillian's sister. The hard one with the will of steel. She runs a pet shop with her husband, Willie, in the main street. Flo and Willie live upstairs with their two little girls, Cissie and Joyce.

"You'll be sleeping downstairs in the shop," Flo warns Robbie.

Upstairs the flat is a soft pink with swirly blue carpet. The shop is neat and bright; rows of cages line the walls and the floor is covered with straw—it's warmer than home. Each morning Flo rolls up the blind on the front window with a terrifying slap and snatches Robbie's blanket out from under him.

"Don't sleep so close to the window. Someone might see you—a customer might see you."

Nobody mentions Lillian. Robbie goes to Cissie and Joyce's school but they refuse to speak to him in public. In the afternoons he goes upstairs with them for bread and jam and Bovril. Cissie is the eldest, with the pinched face of her mother. Joyce is dreamy, with curly hair she winds endlessly around her fingers.

"My mother has hair like yours," Robbie lies one afternoon.

Cissie and Joyce exchange glances. Cissie moves to take his plate.

"What about your dad? Do you know what type of hair your dad has?"

The girls retreat to their room and leave him licking his fingers and stabbing at the crumbs. He can hear them giggling and whining behind the door. Cissie is hissing at Joyce, "Go on, now. Now, *do* it." The door opens and Cissie shoos Joyce out. She sidles across the carpet up to him and to his surprise puts out her hand in the same tentative way the customers reach to pet something for the first time. Her hand brushes the coarse stuff of his shirt; she reaches for the point of his ribs where they have been blown up and out by the nights of wheezing. His own eyes flick down a hundred times a day, but he had thought, in clothes, the bony rise was hidden. Joyce runs backs to Cissie. "There, I did it, see, I did it." They pull the door shut behind them.

"I have a sister, you know," Robbie yells at the door triumphantly. It opens a crack; they can't contain their interest. "What's her name, then, how old—?"

"Is she pretty?" Joyce butts in. "Is she as pretty as me?" She holds her dress out from her legs and spins on the spot. Robbie watches her petticoats fly around and around and tries to find Little Enid's face in his mind. The pink walls of the flat pulse strangely. Warm pee trickles down his legs.

Flo and Willie sell finches and canaries and some expensive budgerigars from far-flung Australia. Willie breeds racing pigeons out the back—"not serious-like, more of a fancier." He shows Robbie Halifax Lady Henrietta. She looks like any other pigeon: gray, nervous, dry-eyed. Willie says she has the body of a champ.

"Isn't she grand, Robbie? Here, you take her, lad, just hold her gentle-like."

She looks harmless in Willie's big hands; he passes her across onto Robbie's chest. They smile at each other and at the bird.

"She likes you, eh?"

They coo at her together. This is what it is like, Robbie thinks—the man and the boy and the bird, the air smelling of fresh straw and no hungry hole inside him. This is what happy is.

He carries a little soil in his pockets. When he is up on the moors with Willie or out on deliveries he collects a sample. He likes to taste the difference of it from place to place. He tells himself it is for his mother—just in case she wants some. Just in case.

One afternoon Robbie is alone upstairs for his Bovril—the girls have gone to dancing class. He takes *Pears' Cyclopaedia* from Willie and Flo's bookcase, flicks to a picture of a strangely large-headed tadpole. Stops to read: *Spermatozoa, the infinitesimal organisms constituting the generating element in male animals.* Reads on. The next entry has a smaller but even more compelling picture. An infant lying on its front, legs froglike out to the sides and a dark, terrible circle in the middle of its back. *Spina bifida, Latin for split spine. A fatal infant deformity where the back is open and components of the spinal column are missing. Seen in the slums and amongst the working class. Poor diet in mothers, esp. lack of grains and fruits (viz. oranges) are thought to be causal.*

Nanna Pett fetches Robbie home. Lillian doesn't come down to meet them when they arrive and Nanna Pett seems nervous. She unloads her basket in the kitchen and unpegs a line of nappies strung in front of the grate. Robbie hears *poorly* and *baby* and *no fire again* but he's not sure of the order. The house seems impossibly small and dark; the stairs are so narrow he has to angle his feet sideways. Surely he can't have grown that much? It's only been a month.

Lillian lies in bed powdering her face. She peers into the mirror of her tiny compact and looks around it at him in exaggerated surprise. She beckons—closer, come closer—until he can see the bundle that lies beside her.

"Our Andrew," she whispers. The baby is small and shriveled. A line of yellow milk has dried into a crust on his cheek but more striking is the red liquid that has leaked through his swaddling and stained the sheets.

"Go on, then, give him a kiss."

Robbie puts his hand out to touch the baby's forehead. His fingernails are rimmed with dirt. Then he darts his head down quickly and manages to kiss more of his own skin than his brother's.

Our Andrew has a soft mewing cry. He sucks at Lillian endlessly. This time of suckling is like time that has closed in on itself. Long, drawn-out afternoons of Lillian in bed and Robbie creeping through the house running his fingers along the window ledges, digging in the soil, painting the step with coal dust and spit, shuffling about, heavy in himself.

Robbie often goes upstairs to Lillian. He sits on the edge of the bed and listens to the baby snuffling as it chews at Lillian's breast. After a little restless sleep Lillian changes the baby. He is always wet, not about the bottom, but from his leaking wound. Lillian dusts some medicinal powder into the hole. It is the same as Little Enid's, a gaping cavity in his back, but on Andrew the wound is higher—centered between the curved bones of his tiny shoulders. It is a deep but perfect circle. Robbie is attracted to it—tempted to lean in and touch it. The wound is the most insistent part of the baby; it is more brightly red, more liquid and more pulsingly alive than his face. Robbie makes his mouth into the shape of the hole and traces his tongue around his lips as if following its contours.

They leave the baby asleep on the bed and Lillian comes downstairs for a bath. She stokes the fire and fills the pans with water. She takes the tin bath down from behind the kitchen door, finds a shard of soap, a towel, and a fresh nightdress. When the water is warmed she places the pans on the floor near the bath with a tall jug and undresses. Robbie sees she is stiff from the baby, stiff from so long in bed. She grips the table as she peels off her socks and underclothes. She fiddles with some pins and undoes a dark rag from between her legs. Robbie recoils. It looks like it is stained with lipstick, a leaking sideways-kiss stain from a pair of large lips, but it is too red, too liquid, too dripping with blood. She climbs tentatively into the bath and sits with her knees drawn up to her breasts.

"Quick now, love, before I'm all iced up."

Robbie pours the first jug over her back and shoulders, watching her skin soften and spread from the warmth of the water. She rubs the hard soap over her arms and shoulders and under her armpits.

"More, Robbie, on my head as well."

The water turns her hair to dark copper with a green shine.

"Did he bite you, then?"

"What, love?"

"Did he bite you, then, on the way out, our Andrew?"

Lillian touches a wet hand to his cheek.

"Oh, Robbie, my love. My love, you have no idea."

Robbie downstairs listening as Lillian sings to the dying baby, her voice as soft and breathy as a child's. Robbie drawing on the back step with a stone—drawing Willie and his pigeons, Lady Henrietta on a tipsy-topsy nest of straw. Robbie thinking about oranges and grains and how much they might cost. Robbie digging up soil with a spoon and sucking on it.

Having a little in his pockets all of the time in case his mother wants some. In case they might sit together once again and share.

11

AFTERNOON TEA WITH DORIS MCKETTERING

It is hard to imagine the Mallee before it was cleared. A scribble of thin trees giving off their skeleton light, birds crying into the dry blue air. Now everything is in boxes. The men of the Mallee toil within the straight fence lines of their paddocks. I have swapped the metal box of the train for the timber box of the house, or the houses of others.

In Elsie Ivers's front room I sit with Lola Sprake, Iris Pfundt, Wilma Noy, and Doris McKettering. They are showing me their school photograph—*Wycheproof District School 1915*. The children are balanced on some invisible scaffolding to make a neat pyramid. There are no uniforms. It must be winter, as they wear heavy jackets in dark colors. Some of the girls have white hair ribbons tied in big floppy bows that fall down to their shoulders. Growing up here seems to have been an exercise in name-swapping. Lola Sprake started out as Lola Noy, Wilma Noy was Wilma Sprake, Iris Pfundt is unmarried, but her sister Doris is now a McKettering. The photograph shows Iris and Doris had two large and handsome brothers, but they were both killed in

France, having run away to enlist at Horsham, where they could lie about their age without fear of being recognized.

Elsie doesn't feature—she grew up in Boort. Although the Wycheproof women say they didn't know her back then, they knew of her brother, who was a champion bicycle racer. He won the Lake Boort picnic race year after year until, at the age of seventeen, he was racing a Buick and the front fender clipped his wheel and dragged him under the car. It seems to me that women should be the ones to carry a name on—we have a better record at continuity.

"We saw your Sister Crock up at Sea Lake and the cooking girl, what's her name?" Doris McKettering turns the conversation to include me in it.

"Mary."

"Mary. Do you know Wilma's husband gave a report on our trip to the train at the Mechanics' Institute? What did Les say, Wilma, that thing about the grass?"

Wilma settles her teacup on her ample lap. "The Better-Farming Train can teach a man to grow *one* blade of grass where *two* grew before."

The women titter.

"But did you hear hear Una Wearmouth?" Lola asks no one in particular. "I think it was in the home economics lecture. The sister's going on about kitchen gardens, how you can use your carrots here and your tomatoes there and Una pipes up, 'What about pig face, Sister? It's the only thing we can grow up here and that's when me husband waters it with the trouser tap!'"

Lola slaps her thigh as she delivers the line. She likes to tell a story. Lola and her husband run the Commercial. She's a good barmaid—a listener and a gossip.

Elsie had warned me about Lola earlier as I helped her put out the teacups. "She's a bit of a gate is Lola. Not much gets around her."

A plate of cakes is passed from hand to hand.

Iris from the library encourages us to try her slice. She looks as desiccated as usual in a knitted peach sundress that droops sadly at the back. "It's a new recipe, this slice, from a book." She gives me a dry smile, all cake crumbs and false teeth.

"I wouldn't have thought there was much on that train that couldn't be found in books."

"I liked the chickens," Doris says. "There were some lovely chickens. The big white ones—wyandottes. And that funny little chick-man. Little Chinese. He was a card. What was his name, Jean?"

"Mr. Ohno—from Japan."

More laughter. Doris blows tea out of her nose and has to dab at her face with a napkin.

"Mr. Oh-no," she gasps between dabs. "His little feet, Jean, his dear little feet. Do you know I dreamt about his little feet? Like a goat's, they were—cloven."

I notice Elsie's face is flushed. She chews her lip and seems torn between wanting to protect me and joining in the fun. I can hear the boys outside doing laps of the house, waiting for cake scraps and the dregs from teacups. I think of Mr. Ohno's pale pink tongue. Of his cool hands with skin so perfect, so without lines or joins or blemishes they look molded from clay. I wonder what I am doing with these women whose lives seem to have neither science nor passion.

I clear my throat to gain their attention. "Actually, Mr. Ohno taught me the art of chicken sexing while I was on the train. It can only be done by those with nimble fingers and a quick mind. I believe he does it for pleasure. In fact, when I did it I found it quite pleasurable too."

The women lift their teacups in unison and drink through pursed lips. Elsie picks at a rumball on her plate and shakes her head. There is nothing left to do but leave.

Doris McKettering stops me at the door. She is large and barrel-chested. All of her curves are outwards but in a firm and quite attractive way. She is the only one to meet my eye.

"My husband, Mrs. Pettergree, fancies himself as a bit of a scientist—although he's pure duffer from what I can see. I'm going to send him over. Ern's his name. Tell your husband to expect him."

Then she pats me gently on the arm and lowers her voice. "And don't fret about fitting in. You'll find your place, lovey. Things just move a bit differently in the Mallee."

I'm well down the driveway when I hear her calling out behind me. When I turn around she's holding a small parcel aloft.

"Jean. Jean. Leftover cakes. Take a box. Sweeten up that man of yours."

12

SOME THOUGHTS ON FENCING

The farm is changing Robert's body. He is hardening. Growing some thicker outer crust to his skin. His hands are bigger. Recently I have woken with his hands on my belly and been momentarily confused, thinking that another man is touching me. Orange soil is seeping into his hands. His face is leaner and a deeper red, while the hair on his arms is so white it is almost translucent. When he scoops water to his face in the mornings, his shirtsleeves rolled high, I am reminded of Sister Crock preparing to bathe an infant—water dripping from her forearms like falling light.

On Tuesday, April 9, Robert sows *Rannee 4H* south of the house. He sows twenty-three acres with three and a half bags. From April 14 to 18, he sows fifty-four acres with eight bags. On May 3 he sows Wether's thirty-two acres with just under five bags. On May 4–6 he sows the west paddock of twelve acres with two and a half bags of *Ghurka*. On Tuesday, April 9, I do out the front room, do out bath, coppers, floors, and safe, Bon Ami windows, clean fireplaces, peg out clothes, clean shoes, test new Trio Brite cleanser, bake mutton, potato and onion pie, make rice custard, milk Folly and take her out to graze in the "long paddock," water the house trees and experimental plants, sew some school pants for Elsie's boys next door, write to Buckleys & Nunn for a Dr. Young's Sanitary Belt, and write to Mary.

I ask Mary for advice about Folly, who often gets the better of me. She is hell to catch and has twice broken into the hay shed and eaten herself sick. Mary has enough on her plate with a new husband and a baby on the way and having to support her parents, as the depression has hit Gippsland hard, but she always writes back.

After lunch I collect Folly from the roadside and tie her under the peppercorn tree for an Insectibane bucket wash to keep the flies away. The chemicals must sting her udder because she skips around and steps on my toes. Robert is bucket washing the car at the same time and I think I catch him smiling at me as I curse Folly and hop about in pain.

Doris sends her husband, Ern McKettering, and he helps Robert with the fencing. One day Ern brings Robert a dog—an eager collie cross with a tufty coat. Ern says the dog is called Jumbo but Robert calls him Will. The dog trails Robert through the paddocks, nose down and shoulders sloping.

I take tea out to the paddocks, where Ern helps Robert dig a deep, long hole to take an old strainer post. The timber, mainly greybox, is still metal hard after many years in the ground. The first layer of soil is hot and smooth. Tiny grains pour over one another. I stand back and watch as Robert uses the back of his shovel to shore it up. He tells Ern of his time at the research station, when he saw men with great skill on the shovel. They were trialing new fencing styles and a team of laborers worked with the students digging holes. He saw a man dig perfect holes, square or circular or even a simple triangle, so smooth and clean and deep they looked like an arrow had been shot into the ground. There was another man who had lost a hand in the war yet he dug with a smooth flicking action, the shovel handle pushed high on his stump. Robert said that these men knew the earth intimately. They knew the exact angle at which to use the blade and the depth and force required.

Later Robert and Ern remove an old dogleg fence—a fence like a living cross-stitch of timber without a single nail or strand of wire. Ern brings Doris over for a look before they tear it down because she's in the local historical society. Doris shakes her head at her husband. She doubts anyone would be interested in a dirty old fence. She spends the afternoon in the kitchen and I find her easy company. She tells me about her three boys who are all up in Queensland working on the sugarcane. She laughs at my stories about Sister Crock and is grateful for advice on the double reinforcing of side seams.

After our evening meal I sit with Robert at the kitchen table. He works on his samples, opening wheat heads on the chopping board to search for bunt and smut. I watch him stroke out the arms of a young plant still pale in its early growing while I hem the curtains for the caravan.

Robert has built the caravan from old fencing timber. It is a timber box on an old plow axle to be hooked behind the tractor. It will mean he can go farther and work longer without having to come back to the house each night. There is a small window at the front and a door at the back. Inside, a narrow bed and a fold-down table. I make him a mattress for his new bed, stuffing kapok into the calico and finishing it in neat blanket stitch. I sew a loop onto a white huckaback guest towel that he hangs on a nail behind the door.

I sit awhile in the caravan each day while Robert is out on the farm. It is cool inside and I must check the length of the curtains, but as soon as I am sitting on the narrow bed I fall into an engrossing daydream. I imagine the caravan is my home— and I imagine how I would live in it. My mind carries each of my essential possessions into the tiny space and thinks of ways to arrange them—my books on a shelf above the door, a drawer for clothes under the bed, a corner for my sewing things. The day-dream gives me such a sense of completeness and satisfaction, I am reluctant to enter the caravan with Robert in case I am drawn into the dream in front of him. I am not sure what it means. It seems to be a wish to be self-contained. There is no space for Robert in the dream, or for science.

"It is your project," I say, when he asks me to hold the tape measure. The caravan will take Robert away from me, but it will bring him closer to the land. I would like this closeness too. I would like to lie in the darkness watching the stars through the little window, listening to the earth as it cools and cracks during the night.

The test run for the caravan is not a success. The floor falls out piece by piece as the tractor does its slow lap around the house. I wave and call to Robert but he can't hear me over the noise. More timber poles are needed so we plan a trip to the pine reserve at Patchewollock. I come along to tend the fires and make our lunch but mainly because of the clearing sale at Day Trap along the way. A whole farm is to be sold up—all machinery, household goods, and a long-bobbin Singer treadle sewing machine in good working order.

Hec Bowd's farm has poor soil. Mallee sand that shifts underfoot and rises with the smallest wind. Robert says Hec Bowd has made terrible mistakes with fallow. He says he let the fields stand for so long between plantings that the soil upped and drifted off by the time he came back to it. Hec was following advice from the *Agriculture Journal*—that long fallow would protect his wheat from field smut. They had three bad seasons and were hanging on. The bank took the final decision.

Robert parks the car under some poplars behind the house. We can see Hec Bowd in the paddock demonstrating his tractor to some prospective buyers. It's a Clectrac crawler that runs on tracks like a tank with a tall air inlet to get above the dust, giving it a military look—like a periscope on a submarine. Robert straddles the fencing wires and walks over to a crowd of men around the tractor.

Mrs. Bowd and her daughter have set up a tea table on the back veranda. They are wearing their best dresses, serving sandwiches and cakes and tea from patterned china normally reserved for a wedding or a christening or Sunday best at least. I have seen them in town before. The daughter, Ollie, is a famous local tennis player. She is strong and spare like her father with a sharp, serious face. I have regularly seen her photograph on the back page of the *Ensign*.

The sewing machine belongs to Ollie. She leads me into the dark sitting room, where it takes pride of place on the circular table. The auctioneer has tied a large tag to it with a number. Ollie runs her hand over the shiny black metal.

"What do you think, Mrs. Pettergree? Dad got it at Swan Hill when he went up with some sheep. It was my eighteenth."

"It's lovely, Ollie. I'll thread it up and run something through it."

Ollie must be in her early twenties by now. She brings me her sewing basket and rummages about for some thread and a bobbin. The basket is made of birthday cards covered in cellophane and sewn together with raffia. The auctioneer's label half covers the face of a white kitten—*to our darling ten-year-old girl . . .*

Ollie watches me trace the thread through the shiny guides and loops.

"Oh, Mrs. Pettergree, do you know I've been doing it the wrong way all this time?" Her cheeks quiver. "It never worked properly, the stitches always pulled tight, and I thought it was me."

She clumps glumly back out to her mother on the veranda.

I look at the photographs on the mantel. Generations of sharp-faced Bowds, Hec's shy young face as a bridegroom, Ollie as a teenager in her Highland dancing outfit.

The auctioneer's voice breaks through from outside. Many more people have arrived. A large crowd is gathered in front of the poplars. The auction men bring box after box of tools and equipment to trestle tables at the front where it is quickly dealt with. Hec Bowd is at the front, nodding and smiling. He tries to engage the bidders—reassuring them of the quality of the goods—but most are embarrassed to meet his gaze. Robert bids on the crawler tractor but is beaten to it by the Bowds' neighbor who, although farming the same treacherous ground, seems to be doing better from it.

There isn't much interest in the sewing machine but Robert is slow to bid. I grip his arm through his coat, urging his elbow up.

"It's a tool too. Just like a tractor. It's a tool for sewing."

Ollie comes over and helps us load it in the back of the car. Then she stands waving to us as we drive away and the dust kicks up around her.

RESULTS FROM THE 1936 HARVEST

This year's sample had a lower bushel weight (59 lbs) than in the previous year. It is hoped this downward trend will be quickly halted and reversed by next season. In accordance with standard sampling procedure a portion of FAQ (fair–average quality) wheat was critically examined and subjected to analysis and a milling test in the experimental flour mill.

The sample is of generally pleasing appearance but the percentage of screenings is considerably higher than usual, due mainly to a high content of broken grain. The moisture content is slightly low, as is the protein content.

Purpose: To measure the quality of wheats grown by Mr. R. L. Pettergree of Wycheproof in regard to high yields of good-colored flour with superior baking quality.

Quality Tests: The Pelshenke figure, which indicates gluten quality (time taken for dough ball to expand under water at temperature; time divided by protein content = quality), is just below average.

Mechanical testing of the physical properties of the dough using Brabender's Farinograph and Fermentograph shows average to poor–average flour quality with acceptable gas-producing power.

LOAF NO.	CRUMB STRUCTURE	CRUST COLOR	LOAF VOLUME	TOTAL
1	6/10	7/10	6/10	19/30
2	6/10	7/10	5/10	18/30
3	6/10	7/10	6/10	19/30
4	3/10	2/10	3/10	8/30
5	7/10	6/10	6/10	19/30
6	6/10	7/10	5/10	18/30
7	5/10	6/10	6/10	17/30
8	7/10	6/10	6/10	19/30
9	6/10	6/10	5/10	17/30
10	6/10	6/10	6/10	18/30

I burned loaf four. If it wasn't an experiment I would have just thrown it away—tossed it out the window to Will. The tendons in my arms ache from kneading.

It wasn't my fault, as the baking technician, that the loaves were not as good as last year, but when I gave Robert the results I felt somehow responsible for them. I placed my hand on his shoulder, but he shrugged it away.

13

BIG BEN FROM THE AIR

According to Robert, Ern McKettering likes his motorcar. His paddocks are crisscrossed with homemade roads. Not just around the edges, but often right through the middle of the crop. He even drives out to the break. Ern invites Robert on a tour of inspection followed by sandwiches from the glove box.

"I fancy I'm a bit of a science man, myself," he tells Robert between bites, "but expert advice never goes astray."

Robert is perplexed by the many small, oddly shaped paddocks. The farm is a gridlock of gates and fences and roads with strips of different crops, even different varieties within the same field. Short-strawed wheats grow next to tall; white varieties mingle with russets. It is clear from the poor state of the crop that Ern is only just keeping it together—that he is knife-edge close to going under.

"Must be hell to harvest."

"True, Pettergree, true. But she's a treat from the air. Dad's idea. He went up in a hot air balloon at the Quambie show and the pilot fella tells him to look down at the artistry of the crops.

Well, he got the idea he could make an actual picture with it."

Robert looks around, trying to discern some sort of shape from the lines of fences filled with crop.

"Hard to pick from the ground. It's Big Ben. He worked from drawings in a book, *Clock Towers of England and Her Isles*. Big Ben was always his favorite."

Robert has no hesitation in dismantling London's famous timepiece. He prepares a farm plan for Ern with regular-size paddocks fenced to soil type. He designs a laneway system to reduce roads and gates and allow easy access for machinery. He explains to Ern how he will be able to drive up the laneway and survey all his crops and paddocks. He likens it to a conveyor belt on a production line. From the laneway all of the farm's components will be visible, checkable, quantifiable.

Ern and Robert peg out the new fences together. It takes weeks, Robert running his eye over the land like a spirit level, Ern following on behind him, always talking, always telling stories. Ern tells of the trip to the sea, his sister's near drowning in the Murray River, the snake that killed his pony, his pocket-money job at the abattoirs bagging dried blood for poultry feed, the mouse plague of 1918, his prize-winning cow—Linga-Longa-Wattle-Speck—the research team that came up from Adelaide and personality tested all of the children at the Wyche School, the Charlie Chaplin film he saw at St. Arnaud . . .

When they reach the farthest fences at the very back of the farm he tells Robert that he'd not really wanted to marry Doris, because he had feelings for her sister.

"Not Iris, of course—never liked a woman without some decent upholstery. There was an older girl, Sarah. She had all this dark curly hair." Ern rocks back on his heels for a minute in contemplation.

"The family bred bulls and hired them out across the district. The bulls were aggressive bleeders. At certain times, if you know what I mean, the girls couldn't venture off the veranda for fear of the bulls. I hadn't really courted her—Sarah, that is. I was still young and so was she, but we had glanced at each other often enough and I fancied there was something between us. One day I heard that a bull had gored and trampled her when she was walking between the chook pen and the house. She was badly injured. They called the bone cart and took her to the big hospital at Bendigo. While she was gone the bulls went stale, all of them off their food and unable to do their duty, if you know what I mean." Ern looks away coyly.

"After a few weeks they brought her back to the house because there was nothing more that could be done for her. She died on that first night back. The next morning they found the bull that had gored her drowned in the dam. He'd just walked straight in. Anyway, Doris sort of stepped into the breach, so to speak—not that I'm complaining."

Ern breaks off to gaze at a cloud.

"What do you think about all that, then, Pettergree? Women and love and all that?"

Robert clears his throat awkwardly. The fencing is just about finished. He asks Ern if they can inspect the dam now. Robert sees water as the biggest impediment to Ern McKettering's farming operation. Ern insists that they drive. The dam is old; its lips are cracked and flaking. The spongy feel of the soil around the rim means it is leaking. Ern and Robert stare into the clayey water.

"How deep do you think?"

Ern picks up a stone and lobs it in. The water swallows it with a plop.

"Less than six feet. They never dig too deep around here. Nothing to fill them with."

Robert starts to unbutton his shirt. He needs a sample.

"Coming in?"

Ern's aging body still holds its muscle well. Robert thinks there is something of the bull about him. Ern cups his genitals in his palm tenderly, more to comfort than hide himself. They edge in sideways, turning the smallest surface to the freezing water.

"Cold enough." Robert grimaces.

"Jesus, Joseph, and Mary." Ern hugs his arms across his chest.

The water is only thigh deep. There is a dead feeling about it. It is heavy water, like the swill that comes off metal. Robert sits on the bottom and manipulates his soil pick underwater. He dislodges lumps of clay, brings them to the surface, and hands them to Ern, who throws them out onto the banks.

"Here." Robert aims too high. A muddy lump hits Ern on the shoulder and slides down his chest.

"Here yourself."

Clay flies. Ern digs with his toes, Robert with his pick. They chase each other, lifting their knees high above the water. Ern beats his chest like a monkey; he has clay through his hair and smeared over his face. Robert spreads the clay over his chest, making patterns with his fingertips. They float on their backs together for a while and then clamber out to dry on the banks.

An ibis lands on the far side of the dam and pokes its beak into the soil cracks. Robert and Ern sit up to watch it.

"Beautiful," Ern says. "Who'd live in the city, eh? You'd have to be a mug."

Robert shifts his gaze from the ibis to Ern.

"I'm only here because of a bird. My uncle won some money on a racing pigeon. Enough for the passage and for university."

Ern smiles broadly and slaps Robert on the back. "A winged benefactor. What a lark, Pettergree, eh?"

They laugh together. Ern drums his feet against the dam wall and the ibis takes off in alarm.

The men dress, gather the equipment, and walk back to the car. Ern sits at the wheel turning the key over in his hand.

"This science stuff, Pettergree. Well, it's got me converted. I'm up for it. Anything you say—I'm up for it."

That afternoon Ern McKettering opens the heavy volume of *Jack's Self-Educator* on the kitchen table and thumbs awkwardly through the lacy pages. He stops at the section on botany and starts to read: "We cannot fail to be struck by the root of the plant. Pull up even an insignificant herb and an extraordinary number of small roots can be observed branching and spreading out in all directions."

Ern takes a crumpled shoot from his pocket. It is small and thin, barely tillering. He holds it upside down, examines the roots, and reads on: "Anyone wishing to spend an instructive but tedious afternoon may be advised to pull up a plant, carefully wash out the roots and measure them all."

The wireless crackles in the background. Something about breeding whippets? He tosses the plant out the window and jiggles the volume dial.

14

A TRAINLOAD OF SUPERPHOSPHATE

Robert collects our mail from the post office. He shows me this letter with a certain pride.

Dear Mr. R. L. Pettergree,

The current world depression has created a looming crisis for our country. The Australian Balance of Payments is heavily in deficit and the flow of capital has been severely arrested.

Prime Minister Lyons plans to overcome these difficulties with an expansion in primary production. Mr. Lyons has made a direct appeal to Australian farmers to GROW MORE WHEAT.

A target of a million more acres of wheat has been set by the Victorian Department of Agriculture. Your expertise in the parishes and towns of Teddywaddy, Wycheproof, Bunguluke, Thalia, Ninyeunook, Cooropajerrup, Carapunga, Narraport, Towaninnie, Tittybong, Nullawil, and Jil Jil is sought.

We ask that you appeal most vehemently to the patriotic natures of the men of your parish. A parcel of promotional goods will follow under separate cover.

C. J. Mullet, B.Agr.Sc.
Victorian Superintendent of Agriculture

Now that the train has been decommissioned, *GROW MORE WHEAT* is the superintendent's new promotional project. The materials reflect his taste for theater—rosettes, bright yellow, slightly crushed, and a poster depicting a farmer in a houndstooth jacket and deerstalker hat smiling from a tiny golden field. *GROW MORE WHEAT* is emblazoned across the hedgerow; blackbirds fly overhead.

Robert plans his approach; the collection of soil data from paddocks in each of the parishes, then the public presentation to each man of the specific equation, including additives and treatments, to be followed. It is a recipe, like one of Mary's, that if followed exactly, in every aspect, will produce the required result. He does our own first:

1936–37 Pettergree, R. L. Wycheproof

160 acres red land from undulating loam through to sandy loam. Spread 90 lbs per acre superphosphate early.

Treat with gypsum at 20 lbs per acre and borax at 15 lbs per acre.

Sow 80 lbs of seed per acre: *Ghurka* and *Ranee 4H*. (Seed to be pickled in a wet solution of bluestone or formalin to insure against take-all, bunt, loose smut, and flag smut.)

Yield: 12 bushels per acre = 1920 bushels in total (0.71% OF THE VICTORIAN WHEAT EXPANSION TARGET)

To write such an equation for every farm hereabouts Robert must know its soil. So we go walking—not for exercise or pleasure, for knowledge.

I feel reinvigorated by this task. Like we are really in it together. We bend over the laces of our boots side by side each morning. I pack a rucksack with lunch and Robert's field equipment: his notebook, a pick, collecting bags, a compass, and a small jar of water. Robert has planned out the routes. We follow the jerky compass needle and mark our progress on survey maps. Sometimes we walk straight out from the house, sliding through the fences in our way; other times we drive to the starting point and leave the car along the road.

We walk in single file through pasture and crops, over fences, across bare ground dotted with tufty native grasses. Robert breaks the crust of the soil with his boots, leaving his print and a spray of fissured cracks around it. The flies are bad in places, especially at the salt lakes, where they swarm at the wet edges of our eyes and mouths. Every fifty feet Robert stops to sample and I am ready with the equipment. He takes topsoil and samples from different depths. I hold the bags open for him and tie them up with string. I pour just the right amount of water into his hand for the elasticity test in which he molds the soil into a sausage then squeezes it from its base to measure the ooze. We tie the sample bags to our belt loops. When we walk they make circles around us like small planets.

The soil is always different, although sometimes there is only the smallest difference—golden brown to golden red, dry to sugary to smooth. I like to watch it pouring into the calico bags and have to curb the impulse to reach out and feel it on my skin. It reminds me of the many fabrics I have handled and know by touch: silk, velvet, rayonelle, chenille, Irish linen, French linen, lawn. My fingers alone could read the warp and weft of the threads.

We often trespass, but avoid confrontation or explanation. If we come upon a house we veer off course until we are well past it and then swerve back to the route. It requires some recalculation. I hand Robert a pencil stub from my pocket. He licks it, taking the numbers apart and putting them together again under his breath. Sometimes we hear dogs barking in the distance or the sound of a car but we have never been stopped or asked our business. Once, startled by rifle shot (some farm children hunting rabbits), we lay down together in a field of oats and held our breath until the danger had passed. (I imagine we looked like the couple in Mr. Vincent Van Gogh's painting *Siesta*—a peasant man and a woman lie asleep amongst the swirling hay. Their working clothes are the same sad, faded blue as the sky but there is such peace in the way that they lie together, not touching, but together in shared exhaustion.)

Lunch is under a gum tree or on the banks of the river. If it is hot we will swim first and then eat so as to be safe from cramps. The water is so bitterly cold it forces me quickly out into the sun. The Avoca is the color of long-brewed tea, its waters oily with shadows from the sugar gums. Robert's body is a patchwork beside it—red arms and face and neck, the rest of him pale and freckled. He stretches out to nap. His breastbone juts out sharply. When we are in bed I like to run my fingers up the sharp rise and then off into the sandy curl of hair on either side. If I hover above him in the dark his rib cage catches the deep sway of my breasts.

I lie next to Robert by the river and watch his chest rising and falling. The sun prickles my face. I stretch my hand out above my eyes and open and close it against the glare. I think about reaching across and touching him, but I am not sure how he would respond. I don't understand this gulf between our bodies and our minds and why it is so hard to move between the two.

Robert grills Ern McKettering for information. He wants rainfall statistics, the exact dates of sowing and harvesting, the seeds planted and bushels produced. Ern says he's got some diaries somewhere, but he can't quite put his hands on them. The shire rainfall records show an average of thirteen inches for the last four years. There is an occasional worrying dip, six inches in 1926, but it seems more aberration than pattern. Robert sits at the kitchen table long into the night calculating and drawing graphs. He drafts an advertisement for the *Wycheproof Ensign*.

> *Farmers of the southern Mallee—do you desire to GROW MORE WHEAT? You are cordially invited to a free lecture on improving profits and productivity. All the money in the bank comes from the soil! Teddywaddy Memorial Hall, 4pm, Saturday, June 18th.*

The meeting is held under the names of the district's dead. The men and boys of Teddywaddy lie in Ypres, Flanders, Rheims, the Somme, Gallipoli and the Dardanelles. And somewhere thereabouts (according to a handwritten sign pinned to the wall) are 236 pairs of socks, 142 pillowcases, 59 handkerchiefs, 40 ambulance cushions, 2 pairs of mittens, and 6 cholera belts sent over by the Teddywaddy Women's Auxiliary.

I put the chairs out, placing them what I hope is an appropriately masculine distance apart. This is only the second of Robert's lectures I have attended.

A car pulls up outside and there is the sound of doors slamming, low talk and laughter. More cars and men arrive. They stand around the entrance to the hall lighting cigarettes and yarning and adjusting their hats. Finally a few start to file inside. Bill Ivers nods at me politely and helps Stan Hercules with the tripod for his camera. Within a few minutes the hall is full of the sound of chairs scraping and men exchanging greetings. I feel overly bright in my yellow patterned dress—like a cheap decoration.

Robert sits at a table on the timber stage leafing through his papers. He wears his dark blue wedding suit and for the first time I notice that his hair is starting to thin. Behind him a crudely painted theatrical backdrop shows Henry VIII in neck frill and knickerbockers holding an ax in a grove of gum trees. Robert stands and clears his throat. He nods to me and I walk to the rear of the hall and pull the door closed. When I turn around he is holding the back of his chair with both hands.

"I have asked you here today at the request of Mr. Lyons and Mr. Hogan. I am a fellow farmer"—there is some coughing and the shuffling of feet—"but I have been called to arms, and I come to extend that call to you.

"Our country, our great country, is in dire need of your skills. The world stands at present on the brink of a serious depression. The pain is already being felt in our cities and towns. We've had a period of wealth and prosperity"—a louder bout of coughing, throat clearing, and shuffling—"during which our government entered into various loans; now, as the economy contracts, the interest on those loans has to be paid."

Robert raises his voice over the noise from the floor. Several whispered conversations have started up in the back rows. He touches a finger nervously to the crease between his nose and mouth and pulls his jacket around him.

"Mr. Lyons plans to overcome these difficulties by an increase in primary production. In Victoria the target has been set at a million more acres. That's a twenty-five-percent increase in area and yield. I believe, and I have irrefutable scientific data to base this belief on, that we here in the southern Mallee can produce that amount alone. Let me demonstrate."

Robert shuffles the papers in front of him. The noise in the hall drops. He finds the sheet and moves to the front of the stage, waving it confidently above his head.

"Mr. Leslie Noy. Are you here this evening, Mr. Noy?"

A plain-looking man in the front row near the aisle stands up. I strain to get a look at him. This must be Wilma's husband and the brother of Lola from the Commercial. Noy's neck and face redden.

"That'd be me."

"From my information, Mr. Noy farms one hundred and twenty acres out at Towaninnie. What would you be getting out there on those red loams, Mr. Noy—six bushels an acre?"

Les Noy looks at his boots. "More like five," he says quietly.

"Well, Mr. Noy, consider this. Manurial trials on red loams demonstrate the efficacy of superphosphate at least one ton per acre, sown early. Add sixty, but preferably ninety pounds per acre of gypsum and several minor elements—zinc sulfate at twenty pounds per acre and borax at fifteen pounds per acre—and you've got a guaranteed increase to eleven bushels an acre. That's over double the production, Mr. Noy."

Les Noy is frowning. "I'm sowing *Bencubbin* and I'm backed up in it. Would I have to be changing over?"

"*Ghurka* and *Rannee 4H* win the yield trials, Noy. If it were my land I'd be changing over, but with this equation you could still make your targets on *Baldmin*, *Bencubbin*, or even *Regalia*—although no man with an ounce of sense would grow a wheat so weak in the straw."

A mouse runs out from under Henry VIII's feet, does a lap around Robert's chair, and exits, stage left. No one else seems to notice but I can't help smiling. It seems like a good omen.

Robert holds the piece of paper out in Les Noy's direction. "Take it, Mr. Noy—it's yours. And there's a similar equation for every man here."

Les Noy comes forward, with some hesitation, but by the time he gets to the stage an orderly line of men has formed behind him. Robert calls out their names like a school roll. There is a break in proceedings as the men read their equations and show them to neighbors and relatives. Robert returns to his seat on the stage although my instinct is he would be better on the floor amongst them. After a few minutes he calls the meeting to order again.

"I propose we agree here today on the bulk ordering of super-phosphate to decrease the unit cost for each—"

"Slow down, Pettergree. Hold your horses. What's this all about? Us putting our hands in our pockets by the looks of it. Which fertilizer company is paying you off?"

Every head turns to the interjector, a thin man in a faded black suit.

"Come clean, man."

I hug my arms to my chest, concerned about Robert's reaction.

He is instantly indignant. "I represent no one and I resent the implication. I stand here as a scientist—if anything I represent scientific endeavor and the improvements it can make to this land. There's no magic here." Robert folds his arms over his chest. "And patriotism. Mr. Lyons asked me to appeal to your patriotism."

Stan Hercules is the first to clap. The others quickly join in. Some men even get to their feet. One or two of the younger men whistle.

Robert motions for quiet. "Down to business. I need a man to take the bulk orders. Is there a volunteer?"

"In for a penny, in for a pound. I'll do it, Pettergree."

Robert gives Ern McKettering a grateful nod and says his name aloud as he writes it down. "Mr. Ernest McKettering."

Ern smiles proudly. He is now the scientist's assistant—an apprentice scientist, perhaps. He taps the toes of his white cricket boots against the hall's timber floor—the action of a man going in to bat. Then he turns and winks at me, as if to say, *That was a bit of fun, eh?*

The day the superphosphate train arrives we are the first at the station, wearing the yellow rosettes pinned to our chests. All of the men of the district are there—some with their wives and children. Boys have been kept home from school to help with the carting; they play marbles as we wait. The sun strikes the glass baubles as they tumble and crack on the platform. The sky is the deepest, brightest blue. We watch a small flock of galahs clean up around the silos across the tracks. They are so common here I hardly notice the beauty of them anymore—their feathers the softest nipple pink.

"It's coming." The boys run down the platform. "It's coming, it's coming."

A dark shape shimmers through the haze and, as it gets closer, solidifies into an engine. The stoker throws his cigarette out onto the line and straightens his cap. We are enveloped in a warm, wet cloud of steam and cinders. Women cover their ears at the scream of the brakes. Robert walks down the line of trucks, clipboard in hand, to check the order. He frees a tie rope on the first tarpaulin and flicks it high over the mound of super-phosphate but it snakes back and catches him sharply across the face. He flinches.

We peer up at the truck. Something is moving on top of the tarpaulin. A filthy bedroll, tied up with a pair of stockings, is thrown down onto the platform. Some of the women look away uncomfortably. Then a man jumps down. He brushes the worst of the gray-green dust from his greasy suit, smiles at us a little sheepishly, hoists the bedroll on his back, and saunters off. As we look down the line of trucks, more and more men are jumping down onto the platform. They are not farming men, or men we would normally associate with the city, but a different sort of men altogether. They have matted hair, ill-fitting clothes. They are men with deep-etched lines of hunger on their faces. Some have battered suitcases, some sugar bags. Several are hatless. One has no shoes—just newspaper tied to his feet with binder twine.

Stan Hercules turns his camera away from the train and takes a portrait of one of the men nursing a thin and mangy kitten. The photograph makes the front page of the *Ensign* under the caption *The Day the Depression Came to Wycheproof*. The kitten, according to the report, died shortly after arrival.

15

SISTER CROCK PROCLAIMS THE BABIES THIN

One night just before the 1937 harvest Robert gets out of bed—
not stealthily, but ordinarily, as if the day has already begun. His
tread is sticky on the linoleum. The screen door sighs and slaps.
Time passes. Perhaps he is tying up the dog, or relieving himself
in the garden, or checking the crop for locusts?

I run my fingers along the walls to find the back door. The
step is still warm from yesterday's soil drift. There is no moon
but the garden is bright with starlight. The beams hit the car,
the outhouse, and the washing line from different angles so that
everything is distorted—bigger, smaller, longer, and flatter, than
in the day. The washing line swings gently. He must have
touched it as he walked past. I check the car and the shed and
walk to the front of the house to look down the track. Some
wheat is broken near the fence in the first paddock. It is a neat
stand of *Gallipoli*, nearly grown, already as high as my navel. I
can see where he has walked in, where his legs have crushed
two valleys in the wheat.

I follow the broken path looking for the shape of him in the distance—the paddock doesn't lead anywhere, just into another paddock of a different variety of wheat and then one of oats. Because I am looking up, not down, my foot touches his leg before I see him and I call out at the surprise of it. He is lying on his side in a half-moon of trampled stalks. "Are you sleeping out here?"

He looks up at me but doesn't answer. I run my foot along the back of his warm calf.

"It isn't working," he says.

"What isn't working?"

He turns his head away. The starlight catches at the corner of his mouth. I stamp the wheat around him to make some room and lie down with my hand around his chest. I hold the prow of his ribs and lie close to him, his body a ship piloting us through the night. Except that he seems to have lost direction, and I am no longer sure where we will end up.

I must have slept a little, next to Robert, for when I wake up the sky has turned upon its head. The giant saucepan is no longer at its jaunty angle but twisted and slipping from the sky.

I lie awake and think of the Better-Farming Train. I remember Sister Crock's saucepan of shiny aluminium that was only to be used to boil water for babies' supplementaries. Demonstration boiling, of course, given to supplement the demonstration baby in cases of extreme heat or loose stools. I remember Mary nodding mechanically when Sister Crock stored the special saucepan in the kitchen and insisted it be kept free from contaminants.

A few days later, when we were at Beulah, we were making Folly her Friday-night treacle pie.

"Here's a good old pot for the treacle!" Mary smiled at me as she placed the shiny saucepan on the stove. We left it for only a minute. Just long enough for Mary to move me into the light near the door to pluck my eyebrows. I stood nervously in front of her. Mary's pale brows were modeled on the startled arches of Lupe Velez. We had seen Lupe and Douglas Fairbanks in *The Gaucho* at Ballarat and walked back to the train together holding hands and sighing at her loveliness.

Too late. Too late for my eyebrows and the treacle. The pan was ruined. We took turns at scrubbing and hacking at it with a butter knife.

"Just hang it up, Jeanie, she won't notice. She only uses it for a doll—really, she's not going to notice."

So we put the saucepan back in its place.

The next day we left Beulah and headed for Birchip. The newspaper was full of babies. A local woman had given birth to triplets—three healthy boys—a credit to womanhood, the medical fraternity, and the whole of the Mallee district. Such astounding productivity in such a small town.

It was the abundance of babies at Birchip that led Sister Crock to change her mode of operation. She looked out at the attendees for her infant hygiene and nutrition lecturette. There were an astonishing number of babies. The Birchip triplets took pride of place in the front row—two in the arms of their sturdy mother, the third held by a teenage girl with long pigtails. The heat was stifling; the babies breathed small hot breaths. Sister Crock rubbed her hands on her apron. "I'll be using a real baby for the demonstration today," she barked. "Pass one up."

Mary had done the preparation—sprayed the pews with Insectibane, boiled the pan of water and left it to cool with the lid on. When Sister Crock poured the foul brown treacly liquid into the demonstration bottle she was as surprised as the women who watched her. There was no explanation or apology. She stared for a moment at the bottle with its slimy lumps of floating treacle, then at the baby in her arms. The contents of the bottle looked much nastier than they were. It did not look like food.

Sister Crock licked her lips briskly. "We will not be doing the demonstration feeding today. It is too hot. But it is the perfect time for a weigh-in. Correct weight of the infant is of great importance. Mothers, strip your babies, please."

It was a military-style operation. The naked babies were handed up to Sister Crock and back again via a human chain. The carriage filled with a noisy wailing, the women's hands were wet with sweat and tears. Sister Crock's scales bobbed and dipped and only halted when she bent to rule another column in her record book. Sweat marks spread across her uniform like a tide, starting at the underarms.

The event pushed the harvest from the front page of the *Birchip Advertiser*. SISTER CROCK PROCLAIMS OUR BABIES THIN ran the headline. The story reported that even the Birchip triplets were of lower birth weight than a random sample of city babies conducted by the Melbourne Royal Children's Hospital.

"Thin," said Sister Crock, "is the enemy of every healthful mother."

Sister Crock, who had never married or had a baby. Who had never worn trousers or swum naked in a river. Who, on my engagement, had given me a private lecture on "marital hygiene" in which she referred euphemistically to "flowers" and "stethoscopes." What would she think of me spending the night with my husband in the wheat?

We wake in the noisy half-light to the pernickety tread of ants and the tearing jaws of leafhoppers. And something else. The sound of movement beneath the earth. The roots of the wheat pushing through the soil? Or the scratchings of mice?

Robert reaches his hand over my head into the stems and snaps one clean. A tiny brush drags at the back of my calf. A pause. The stem bends under folds of cotton and finds its path again, circling my thigh. Further rucking up of my nightdress, the muffled feel of it through cotton on my buttocks then skin again—the small of my back. Upwards, slowly, tracing the triangles of my shoulder blades. Then the sound of him moving behind me and his sharp inhalation as he pushes the nightdress over my head. Turning me over—a hand on either side of my belly, my hair twisting and spraying a mist of dirt and wheat stubble across my face and chest. Somewhere in the distance a magpie warbles. The stem again; brushing the fronts of my thighs, sweeping around my navel. Higher. Dragging through the moistness of armpits. The brush's head now bent and crushed. A fast figure eight over the large circles of my breasts, slower over the areola, slower still over the nipple's eye, a gentle swabbing. I can feel the valves of my heart opening and closing, opening and closing.

He watches the path of the brush intently. It curves up my neck, climbs my chin, traces the ridge where skin becomes lips. Quickly, impatiently, he pulls back and starts again at my belly, drawing a sharp, straight line into the curly hair of my sex. He traces the very edge of the soft mound and then dips in, nudging the lips apart in a slow prising.

Things are slipping. I reach out over my head and grab a handful of stalks. The soil cracks around me as I hold on to them and pull. Robert dips himself into me, coating his fingers, then his penis, jutting and rubbing. The brush has fallen across my face. Tongue stretching, I pull it into my mouth. As he slides into me I grind it between my teeth—it tastes of wheat meal and my own yeasty oil.

RESULTS FROM THE 1937 HARVEST

This year's sample has a lower bushel weight (54 lbs) than previous years'. The gains expected through the adoption of superphosphate have been more than offset by the severe mouse plague. In accordance with standard sampling procedure a portion of FAQ (fair–average quality) wheat was critically examined and subjected to analysis and a milling test in the experimental flour mill.

The sample was variable with some bright, plump grains of pleasing appearance and some smaller and paler grains. Contamination with rodent feces was evident. Protein and moisture content is substandard.

Purpose: To measure the quality of wheats grown by Mr. R. L. Pettergree of Wycheproof in regard to high yields of good-colored flour with superior baking quality.

Quality Tests: The Pelshenke figure, which indicates gluten quality (time taken for dough ball to expand under water at temperature; time divided by protein content = quality), is below average. Mechanical testing of the physical properties of the dough using Brabender's Farinograph and Fermentograph shows below-average flour quality with gas-producing power in the low-to-normal range.

LOAF NO.	CRUMB STRUCTURE	CRUST COLOR	LOAF VOLUME	TOTAL
1	6/10	6/10	5/10	17/30
2	6/10	5/10	5/10	16/30
3	6/10	5/10	5/10	16/30
4	5/10	4/10	5/10	14/30
5	6/10	6/10	5/10	17/30
6	6/10	5/10	5/10	16/30
7	5/10	6/10	5/10	16/30
8	4/10	5/10	6/10	15/30
9	6/10	5/10	6/10	17/30
10	6/10	6/10	4/10	16/30

They ate the grain from its bags, inside out. They ate the Ford's upholstery. They ate the eyelids of a sleeping baby. They ate the kitchen curtains. They ate every chaff bag in the district. They did not eat the superphosphate.

They lived in tunnels and caverns and great moving nests under the ground. Children held them by their tails and smashed them on the ground or stood on them or burned them or drowned them in buckets and kero tins and casserole dishes. They stopped being many small things and became one big thing.

No one said *mouse*. Mouse was too soft, too small, too frail. We said *mice*. Mice. Lice. Vice. I saw one run over Robert's head, skid down the pillow, and leap for the floor as he lay next to me in bed. I let him sleep.

They ate the pink gloves Mr. Talbot gave me. They ate two of Robert's notebooks. I would not have blinked if they had carried Folly away. They wore her out. She stamped her feet all night long to stop them climbing up her legs.

When they had eaten everything they died, but we could still smell them. Even when all the corpses were gone—burned to cinders. The fetid perfumed smoke of dead mice hung around. It was always there—behind every other smell we reached for.

16

DROUGHT

We dream of baths. Of that delicious moment when skin goose-pimples and prickles and then slides smooth under a film of water. Hot baths. Cold baths. Mottled river baths. Baths slow with heady oils and perfumes.

Doris McKettering tells me that she dreams of the New Radox Bath, which, for two shillings and sixpence, oxidizes away fat. In her mind's eye she sees herself rising from the fizzing waters no longer a jolly tugboat but a racing yacht. She keeps the New Radox Bath in her vanity box under the bed along with some Venetian Muscle Oil for sunken tissues and a Celadonna Knit Artificial Silk Nightgown. All on hold, but for rain.

Iris Pfundt reports a rush on books about the seas and oceans, about polar exploration and the snow-covered lands of Canada.

The *Ensign* records the days without rain and runs articles on stock losses and how a local housewife is saving water by boiling potatoes in beer or using wool fat to clean her infants.

The government sends water trains.

Folly gives milk every second day. She grubs around for feed and is a Houdini with the gates. She eats two pairs of socks off the line and the bristles from the house broom. If I'm late with her hay she calls for it incessantly and stamps up and down the fence digging a tunnel with her hooves.

I purchase Robert new cooling, superabsorption asbestos insoles for his boots. Several local farmers have asked him to buy back their superphosphate. Without rain there is no point in spreading it.

I cut my hair short to save on washing. A short straight bob that grazes my ears. When I look down the hair falls forward into my face. It feels light, like the touch of fingers, and for the first few days, until I get used to it, I imagine Mr. Ohno's cool fingers stroking my forehead.

Robert hasn't said anything about my hair. He doesn't say much at all. Everything has dried up between us.

"Now isn't that a beauty? Isn't that the roundest, most beautiful thing you've ever seen?" says Ern McKettering.

Doris rocks backwards on her heels and smooths her apron over her middle. "Ern, don't be a goose. She was a purely economic decision. She's a whatsit—an insulator. One good rain and we'll be right."

I smile at Doris. Robert rubs his chin and looks at the ground. Ern can't drag his gaze from his new water tank. It is the biggest ever seen in the district. And here, on its side, attached to a knot of struts and ropes and pulleys, it is indeed a very beautiful vessel. The galvanized sheen is so fresh and new it glows blue in the morning light. Each corrugation casts a perfect shadow on the dip below so the tank looks somehow alive and undulating.

Robert takes off his jacket and slowly rolls up his sleeves. He is here to advise on the best spot for the tank stand. Ern ordered the tank after one of Robert's spiels. It was the insurance spiel about planning and managing drought—about insuring against the lack of rain in the same way ships insure against hitting a whale. "We don't need to insure with money. We need water. If every farmer had a big enough tank to see them through several years—enough even for irrigating—we'd be shored up for as long as it takes."

Ern had nodded. It made sense. He told Robert about a book his mother read to him as a boy. A squirrel that played the fiddle all summer instead of collecting nuts. The tiny creature nearly died in a puddle of icy snow until his neighbors took pity on him. No squirrels here, of course. But Robert might be right. Maybe the Australian farmer lacked the collecting and insuring ethic—always expecting his mates to pull him out of a tight spot.

When Robert heard from Ivers and several other sources that the biggest bloody tank they'd ever seen was waiting in the railyards for collection, he rubbed nervously at the deep groove that ran between his nose and mouth. That evening we drove into town and sure enough there it was. A brand-spanking-new thirty-thousand-gallon tank. And there was McKettering, hands in pockets, hat tipped back, showing it to Don Busby from the bank as if he'd given birth to it.

Finding the best spot for the tank and planning its installation isn't an everyday job. Which is why we are here on a Saturday and why the men are wearing their good shirts and I'm to help Doris with the lunch for after.

Robert does slow laps around the tank. His face is bunched in concentration.

"Right, McKettering." He slaps his hands against his thighs. "This is an exercise in the science of loads. You will be aware that the ancient Egyptians built pyramids with the most rudimentary of tools. Force and fulcrum equals load. That's all we need—history, knowledge, and a piece of paper."

Ern is delighted to have Robert take control and even happier to be given an instruction. "Right, Pettergree. Paper it is."

Doris and I follow Ern into the house, where he pulls out every drawer in the kitchen before she opens a biscuit tin and hands him a pad of writing paper.

"Housewives' mouse-proofing tip number one." She smiles at me. "Tea, Jean, lovey?"

While the men work on the tank Doris boils the kettle and gives me the news from her boys. I notice that she adds the milk to the cups before the tea. I think about my experiment with Robert in the cookery car. At the time I thought it was some sort of metaphor for us—to prove or disprove the success of our partnership. It didn't occur to me then how important a few cups of liquid could be. Or the significance of the vessel in which the liquid is contained.

In the face of all this we celebrate the Queen's birthday with a jazz picnic on Mount Wycheproof. Banjo Andrews and the Wycheproof Footwarmers have returned from playing on the radio in Melbourne. They wear dinner suits at midday. Flora

May and her sister Nell sit on wicker chairs at the front playing twin banjo mandolins, their hair blowing in a rare breeze. The whole town is out—adults perched on the odd-shaped boulders, children swarming on the lower slopes. I sit with Elsie Ivers on an old rug of Douglas tartan. She's hard-pressed swatting flies and keeping the boys out of the picnic basket. Lola Sprake from the Commercial comes over for a chat. She makes a point of mentioning that her sister-in-law, Wilma Noy, couldn't be here as Les has had to sell the car, and gives me a long, hard look.

The wind is rising. Robert is off talking to McKettering. They are watching some young men get ready for a bicycle race down the mountain. I watch as Robert's hat is swept from his head in a strong gust. The scraggly gums are shedding their leaves like confetti on the crowds. The May sisters raise their heads and stare up into the sky. Their light and twangy music rolls over the sides of the tiny mountain like mist.

The first drops of rain pass without notice. It is the wind that has caught our attention. I feel a tiny splash hit my hair and settle warmly on my neck. Then more, my head is prickling with it. The older Ivers boys return with little Percy; he is just walking and has never seen rain before. He holds out his wet-smattered hands to his mother in astonishment.

Everyone rushes for the cars and buggies. Ern and Doris wave cheerfully to us as they pass: "I reckon me tank will be full before we get home." Ern grins. The dust and rain on his cricket boots has turned them streaky orange.

People return to their farms and houses and, like us, take every vessel, every pot, pan, basin, and bowl outside to be filled. Children dance to the syncopated sound of raindrops hitting enamel. Thunder rolls and cracks overhead; it seems to be threatening a downpour. But then, after less than half an hour, the rain stops. The gray sky rolls away and is replaced by high white cloud—pretty but empty. A cruel false alarm.

The only rain comes in Mary's next letter. Flash flooding in Gippsland strands her in hospital for an extra week with her new baby. She says that at least the youngster will feel at home—exiting one watery world to arrive immediately in another.

A few slow, dry afternoons later, Les Noy comes by on a bicycle. His face is very sunburned. I offer him a drink. He shakes his head. He asks for Robert, but I'm not sure whereabouts on the farm he is, or what time he'll be back. Les says good-bye, and I assume he's left until I hear a noise against the side of the house. I open the window and see him stacking some bushels of poor-looking wheat under the eaves. He sees me watching him and points to the wheat.

"Tell him that's an acre." He takes a piece of paper from his pocket, screws it up, and throws it on the feeble stack. "He can have his bloody equations back too. Fat lot of good they did me."

17

MR. FROGLEY BLOWS IN WITH THE DRIFT

Fences mark one man's crop from another but they have no power over the land itself. They can't contain the sandy soil that blows and blows in vast rolling clouds most afternoons. The soil storms rush through trees and dams and herds of anxious sheep, who lie down to sleep thinking it is night. Soil clouds roll right through the house, in at the back, out at the front. There is always soil in our cups when I pour the morning tea.

AGRICULTURE JOURNAL, VICTORIA, MARCH 1938
The Sand Drift Relief Committee reports that claim forms should be obtained from post offices. Claimants are advised to complete both the pink and the blue form and attach them to the yellow form. An entirely separate claim must be made on the green form where a share farmer is party to a share-farming agreement. In order to facilitate payments, and to obviate unnecessary correspondence and delay, all writing must be in ink, and incomplete claim forms will not be accepted.

The soil is so high against the door of the machinery shed Robert has to dig the tractor free each morning. Will's kennel has been buried. He now sleeps in the car, which is stranded, soil as high as the running boards.

The government sends a gang of laborers to shovel the soil that has built up in dams and channels and along fence lines. The laborers started at Swan Hill some months ago and are working their way down to us. When the gang arrives at Ivers's next door, Robert insists on going out to help. I cook Cornish pasties with a knotted pastry top for a handle—just like the miners' wives, except my concern is for dirt above the ground rather than below it. Robert digs the car free and leaves with a gunnysack on the front seat, Will and the tools on the back.

Later, as I am brushing the dirt from the windows in my apron dress, Folly starts to bellow. I think Robert must be back and check the shed for the car but it isn't there. The dust has risen in Folly's paddock. She is trotting towards the house—she doesn't usually trot anywhere—but in the distance I can make out a figure moving in front of her. A man is walking across the paddock with Folly close on his heels, pushing his pockets with her nose. He sees me and waves. A cloud of flies rises and disperses and then settles again around his outstretched hand, which he is holding at a strange angle, as if it is injured.

When he reaches the fence Folly gives up on him and heads back to the shade. The man's clothes are filthy. His rabbit-felt hat has a tide of sweat stains rising from the crown. I stand still on the back step and watch him climb through the fence. I'm unnerved by a strange man appearing so brazenly at the back door but his face, when I can see it more clearly, is reassuringly old and ordinary.

"Your mister said you could help me with this." He shakes the fly-covered hand towards me. "Frogley. Me name's Neville Frogley." He takes off his hat and smiles. His eyes flicker quickly over my body. "Got a touch of the Barcoo rot in me hand and she's slowing me up a bit."

The man is short, but strongly built. His hair is flat and dark, most likely dyed, and he has a beautiful pair of false teeth—small and elegant, as if they were made for a woman. I retie my apron strings firmly and invite him into the kitchen. He holds the back door open, leaving his arm outside for a final shake, then quickly pulls it in. I fetch an enamel basin with water and throw in a handful of salt. He lifts his hand onto the kitchen table and I flatten his fingers back gently. The rot—an infection caused when the skin is broken and open to the flies—has eaten a deep channel across his palm; part of the heel of his hand has been worn away. I splash it with salt water and blot it dry with a tea towel. He watches me as I fetch an old sheet and rip it with my teeth.

"Is it hard work?" I ask him, picking a cotton thread from my tongue.

"Government gangs are as hard as it gets. Not much else around, though. And that's the Mallee for you, eh? Hard work and no reward."

The pretty teeth make a slush of his s's. He looks around the kitchen at my labeled tins and boxes, at my lists of oven temperatures and my cleaning rota pinned to the wall. He looks through the glass that covers the kitchen table to the menu underneath with the list of meals and ingredients; Monday through Sunday—roast, of course, with a fruit or egg pudding depending upon availability. He looks at the long bench under the window—Robert's notebooks and samples, his microscope, jam jars full of soils and seeds and fertilizers, boxes of slides.

"I recognized your husband. Can't think from where, though. Ink slingers, are ya? You and the mister?"

"Ink slingers?" I soak the bandages and squeeze the excess brine into a basin.

"Teachers. You know—ink slingers, pen pushers."

"No. We're farmers—like everyone else, Mr. Frogley."

He snorts and jerks his head around. "So you're from around here, then?" he asks.

"I'm from the city originally."

"Haven't seen you there," he says.

"In Melbourne?"

He rolls his eyes. "Swan Hill. Swan Hill is the city around here."

I fold the bandages in a wad over the wound, packing them in tightly. He grimaces.

"I come to Wyche sometimes. Played footy here way back and I like to catch up with me mates."

I nod.

"There were always them small parrots here—red-rumped fellas. We'd come off at half-time and they'd be all over the field scratching about in the divets, pulling up onion grass. Even hung about when we played, they did. Like playing in a storm of feathers it was." He looks across at me. "So I suppose you've seen 'em, then, suppose you see 'em all the time, them parrots?"

"No. I've never seen them."

He snorts.

I fetch my sewing basket and thread a needle using the faded blue of his shirt as a backdrop, then I stitch the layers of bandages together. It is a test of accuracy—my head bent close in front of him—to pick up the cloth but not the flesh.

"I think it's the wheat," I say. I don't know where this thought came from but suddenly it seems somehow true, obvious even, that with more wheat there will be fewer animals and that the small creatures—frogs, skinks, birds—will be the first to go.

"Well, you've got enough of it," the man says. He looks around again. Stares for a minute at the jars of soil and then slaps his good hand on the table.

"That's it. He's the soil chappie from the farming train. That's where I seen him before, down at Avoca. I was on me way back from a fishing trip in Gippy."

"My husband is an agrostologist—a specialist in soil and crops."

The man snorts. "He's a bloody specialist, all right. He was a bloody specialist with my money if I remember rightly."

I lean in towards the stitching. I'd like to know more but it would be disloyal to Robert to ask.

A fly bangs angrily against the kitchen window. I can feel the man's eyes on me—he's looking through my thin dress with no sleeves and deep V-neck, which is meant for a blouse underneath if it wasn't so hot.

"My eldest looks a bit like you, but she's got one of them permanent waves. Spends her life looking after it."

There is a glass of Folly's milk still on the table from breakfast. It is thin and silvery—with a cinnamon dusting of soil. He places a finger in it and paints the milk across my cheek. I cringe.

"Good for the complexion. That's what the girls say."

I glance up at him—the teeth are somehow repulsive, like my sour aunt's mouth transplanted into a man's face. I wipe my cheek with the selvedge from the sheet and tie off the thread.

He looks a little nervous, like he wishes he hadn't touched me, but then his face hardens again.

"Well, the Mallee's finished anyway. You'll all be sold up. You should never have come out here in the first place, missus. It ain't the place for the likes of you."

The wind is rising outside. I can hear soil moving against the side of the house and I'm pleased to be sending him out into it.

The drift that blew in Neville Frogley, or maybe the drift we battled the days and weeks before or after, made its way into the city. Melbourne—the real city, that is.

In a lunch shop on Collins Street clerks are perched on a row of stools, their briefcases standing to attention like faithful working dogs, when the sky suddenly starts to darken. Some of the men—the younger types—run out into the street, the shop bell jingling in their wake. The sky is in turmoil. A great orange cloud moves overhead, skirting the tops of the tallest buildings.

"It's a tropical storm."

"It's an alien invasion."

"It's the Russians."

"It's a fire at the paint shop."

"It's the end of the world."

An older clerk polishes off the sandwiches his friends have left behind, chewing the crusts resolutely—if he is to die, let it be while eating—and stumbles on the answer. The great orange cloud is soil. The very soil that nurtured the seed that grew the wheat that made the bread he chews upon.

For three days a freak wind takes whole paddocks of Mallee soil up and away to Melbourne, where it rains upon lush green lawns and stains the underclothes of the city folk. They are outraged. There is an increase in nasal catarrh, the discharge a disturbing liquid pink. Housewives write to the newspapers demanding compensation for their ruined washing. One woman claims the soil that came through her window contaminated a summer's worth of fruit she had cooling in jars.

Robert scoffs as he reads the newspaper reports: "Three days of discomfort. Tell them to come and live here for a year. Tell them to come and breathe a few lungfuls of our fine country air."

When the soil storms blow themselves out I walk Folly down to the river in search of some green pick. The Mallee has gusted itself upside down. In the pure state of nature the root of the plant lies beneath the soil, not above it. But here the drift has blown the soil away, several feet of it, so the roots of the Mallee scrub sit up, exposed, like the unclothed bodies of men and women. There is something obscene in the way the tripod legs meet the torso, often with dangling root hairs or a hanging tuberous growth.

18

WING FOOK'S MARE

Robert has never been into horses but the sand drift is making tractor work impossible. He asks the Chinese hawker Wing Fook to look out for a steady mare and a week later Fook appears at the door. Robert greets him with a riddle: "What is the Mallee, Mr. Fook?"

Fook smiles obligingly, showing his tannin-stained teeth. He has no answer.

"A small area of land surrounded by mortgage." Robert delivers the punch line then looks around at the dry paddocks. "If it wasn't so sad it'd be funny."

Fook brushes a fly from his mouth. "Yes, velly funny, Mr. Petteygee." He is keen to change the subject. "Mr. Petteygee, I bring that horse for you."

They walk out to Fook's cart. A swaybacked mare is tied to the rail. Robert looks her over—a thin, washed-out chestnut with a bitten-off tail.

"Is she sound?"

Fook shrugs. "I think. But she not look so good."

They bargain. Robert can't afford the horse but he doesn't want the Chinaman to see what he's come to. Things are dire but he has his pride.

The mare is placid. She follows Folly around. She walks with her head down, sometimes bumping her nose on the ground. Until one day when she is left on her own. Then she walks blindly through a barbed-wire fence. She cuts her chest and neck to shreds and bleeds to death.

It dawns on Robert bitterly. "She not look so good" meant she could not see.

RESULTS FROM THE 1938 HARVEST

This year's bushel weight of 47 lbs is the lowest for the past four years. A poor season created extremely taxing conditions for growers. Additives, where used, have improved yields marginally, but not enough to offset their cost.

In accordance with standard sampling procedure a portion of FAQ (fair–average quality) wheat was critically examined and subjected to analysis and a milling test in the experimental flour mill.

The sample is noticeably smaller and duller. Rust is evident. The amount of weed seeds (saffron, thistle, barley, wild oats, etc.) is higher than in last year's sample. The moisture content is below normal, as is the protein content.

Purpose: To measure the quality of wheats grown by Mr. R. L. Pettergree of Wycheproof in regard to high yields of good-colored flour with superior baking quality.

Quality Tests: The Pelshenke figure is poor. Mechanical testing of the physical properties of the dough using Brabender's Farino-graph and Fermentograph shows average flour quality with slightly lower than acceptable gas-producing power.

LOAF NO.	CRUMB STRUCTURE	CRUST COLOR	LOAF VOLUME	TOTAL
1	5/10	5/10	4/10	14/30
2	4/10	3/10	5/10	12/30
3	6/10	5/10	4/10	15/30
4	4/10	4/10	4/10	12/30
5	5/10	4/10	5/10	14/30
6	5/10	5/10	3/10	13/30
7	4/10	4/10	4/10	12/30
8	4/10	5/10	4/10	13/30
9	5/10	3/10	4/10	12/30
10	4/10	3/10	5/10	12/30

The loaves are smaller, meaner, and slightly orange, as if they have taken on the color of the soil.

I fold the table of results and place it in Robert's notebook, then I wrap four of the loaves in damp tea towels and take them over to Elsie next door. She is carting bathwater out to her rose-bushes, although they look all but dead. Her boys run along behind her catching the drips in a kerosene tin and transferring them carefully to a dirt cricket pitch they are preparing out the back. The older boys use their mulga-wood bats to smooth the few drops of water over the dirt, but it soaks away instantly. They don't seem to notice. They tell me they are making a "sticky wicket" in the style of last summer's test played at the Sydney Cricket Ground, where Mr. Donald Bradman led our team to victory against England and where the wicket, it was said, had the properties of a sticky dog.

19

THE DEATH OF FOLLY

This morning, when I stretched up to find my face in the rectangular mirror over the bathroom sink, my eyes were blue. I turned my head from side to side watching the light film over them, thinking it was a trick of reflection. But from any angle, singularly or together, they are blue.

I unpick the thread from the corner of the cot sheet and try to match the new color in Super Sheen but the blues are too sweet—cornflower or china—or too strong—royal and navy. The new blue of my eyes is flat and streaked. It is the blue of burning kerosene.

The sheet is for Mary's baby. An outline of Folly's face and my own half-turned towards each other like newlyweds. Across the top, in spoke stitch, I have embroidered GREETINGS FROM THE MALLEE. When I post the sampler to Mary there will be a letter with it breaking the news that Folly is dead.

If Mary were here I would have told her how it happened many times over. By telling it, always starting or finishing at a different place, focusing on each small piece of it, I would somehow have etched it into my mind. Whenever I thought of it again it would have been there—a solid moving picture of memory. Without Mary, and with no one else to talk to, it has been laid down without words and is forever getting up again and disturbing me with some new detail.

Now it is my sandals. I remember them filling with twigs and stones as I run across the fallow paddock. It is so hard to run on this slippery bed of burnt dirt. Folly is in front of me, lying bloated on her side in the barbed shade of some stunted gums by the river.

I'm running and slipping. Stopping to hop and shake my feet. All the while Folly is in front of me. I don't seem to be getting any closer. Her back moves up and down with my breath. I limp the last few yards on the sides of my feet and kneel beside her, smoothing my hands across the flat of her haunches, across her belly snapped tight. Her front legs are bent at the knee as if she is having a cantering dream. Her ears are thin and frayed at the edges, the veins still blue with blood. But I can see too that her sheen is gone and her chest has sunk unnaturally into the dirt. Her tongue, a nasty mottled purple, protrudes from slack lips. I think for a second that I see one of her eyes move—that she has winked at me, like Abe the cat—until I lean in closer. A fat clump of maggots slides across the lake of her eye. My breath is solid and hard to move and I think, Not now, Folly, not now, please, don't be dead now.

Leave that. Go back further. Go back a few more days to the first time she was down. Remember how her milk was tinged with green and I had to coax it out of her. How I asked Robert to look at her.

"Just look, you don't have to do anything, just look at her."

"It's hardly my specialty—scrub cow. I said you shouldn't have brought it here."

I ripped the cloth off the table in fury and stood with it flapping in my hand.

"Just look at her!"

I remember the whole dragging length of that next day. Checking Folly every hour, watching the horizon for the tractor. Not cleaning or cooking. Sitting on the step eating a whole shepherd's pie with my fingers. Finally, at dusk, Robert comes back in. I am holding a bucket of treacle mash up to her.

"How long has she been this bloated?"

"A while, I think. I thought she was putting on condition. But this last week she can hardly move."

He reaches for her udder and squeezes it hard. She groans and lifts a hind leg in protest.

"Stinking weed. She's eaten a bellyful of stinking weed. She's chockablock with poison gas. Most likely it'll kill her."

"Can't you do anything?"

"Try to pump her. If that doesn't work we'll have to stick her, which will probably kill her anyway."

I remember the next morning. Getting up early to walk to Ivers's for a bicycle pump. (It occurs to me here, at this point in the retelling, that Robert could have driven me the evening before. He could have got the car out or gone himself and if she'd been pumped sooner, perhaps she would have lived.)

There are three large paddocks between the two farms. A mass of tiny green locusts attach themselves to my yellow dress as I walk. One of the Ivers boys hangs upside down in a nectarine tree near the house. I lick my teeth and try to smile at him. "Is your mother about?" He hangs still for a minute, not wanting to believe I can see him, and then swings down to the sound of tearing fabric that we both ignore.

"Yeah, I'll look."

Elsie is in the washhouse, where she's up to the blue and pleased to see me. I wring and rinse her last load while she searches for little Percy to send into the paddocks to find his dad, who will be able to put his hand on the pump straightaway. (Unlike Elsie or the bigger boy, who don't even bother to look.) We peg out together while we wait. Elsie looks at me sharply as she shakes out a towel.

"At least you come when you need something. It's a start."

I am reluctant to handle her husband's large underpants and fish around in the basket for something safer.

Still no pump. We move into the kitchen and I help her chop onions and peel hard-boiled eggs for a new, modern recipe she is trying for the first time. Spaghetti Beehive. Elsie reads the directions to me from the latest edition of *Woman's World*: "'An intriguing and economical concoction. Line a mold with cooked spaghetti arranged in beehive fashion.'"

Elsie is using a shallow pan in place of the mold—more a car tire than a beehive.

"'Fill with sliced rabbit, tomato, sliced hard-boiled eggs. Firmly pack dissolved gelatin in hot stock and pour into mold. Chill. When set, serve upside down on a plate surrounded by lettuce.'"

There's nothing green or leafy in the Mallee. I wonder what she'll use for lettuce.

Leave the beehive. Robert wouldn't have eaten it anyhow.

We don't eat rabbit. It's one of Robert's principles. Pests are the enemy and eating them encourages laxity in control. Skip over the search for little Percy, who has found the pump and taken it to his lair of broken fruit crates under the house. Ignore the older boy, the nectarine-tree boy who has been picking the remaining locusts off my dress and crushing them between his fingers, and who now, even though all the locusts are gone, continues to rub his hand up and down my leg.

Get home at last, with the pump. Wave it at Robert like a baton. This time he gets down from the tractor and comes to help. Hold Folly's head while Robert does this foul thing to her, forcing the air back up through her teats to clear the first milk and make a vacuum through which the stinking gas can escape. He uses one hand to make a seal between the valve and her teat and the other to operate the pump.

"Hold her, Jean, hold her still."

I'm trying. We dance about, Robert and I connected to each other by a rope and a struggling cow and a hissing pump. There are embarrassing noises—balloons squirting and deflating. Robert isn't hopeful; he says there's nothing more to do but wait.

Back to the sandals. To the fallow paddock. I find a smoother path to run on. The twin tracks of the tractor wheels are on either side of me. I am running in the path made by something dragged behind them. Something large and heavy.

Robert dragged her here to burn. The chains had dug into her hind legs so deeply he cut them off with an ax to free them. He lit her with a can of kerosene at dusk, when the wind had died down. I sat on the back step and watched the blue flame burn through the night.

20

A Dodgy Merchant and His Dog

For some it is not the drought or the mouse plague or the sand drift or even agricultural science that brings them undone, but economics—the money science. I piece this together from what Doris gets out of Ern and from Lola at the Commercial and the other women whose husbands sign up for a forward contract.

Ride the market, ride it hard.
Enter a forward contract.

It was too mystical an equation for Doris. Ern tried to explain it at the kitchen table.

"Imagine the tablecloth is a paddock. Right now it's bare, nothing there, but it has the potential to produce something valuable."

"More tablecloths?" Doris quips.

"No. No. It's an example, Dodee. The tablecloth is the paddock. The paddock without wheat, but considering everything—our previous harvests, the weather, the price of wheat in Europe—it has the potential to produce so many bushels of

Australian Standard White at fair to average quality. Where are you going?"

"To get the good tablecloth. It'll look more like the wheat."

Ern watches Doris as she unfurls the best linen cloth, waving it like a flag in front of her. The soft pink flesh of her arms jiggles above the elbow. She is smiling a small pretty smile. The cloth is smoothed, the salt and pepper shakers repositioned in the middle of the paddock. Ern continues.

"So when is the price of wheat better? Now, when there is nothing on the market? Or the end of next summer, when every cockie in the country has stripped and bagged and can't buy next year's seed until he sells?"

Doris takes a punt: "Now?"

"Exactly. We are going to sell before we've even planted. We are going to sell our potential."

Doris strokes the tablecloth. "So it's a good idea?"

"It's a ripper."

"You don't think you should write to the boys and see what they think?"

"Pah! It's wheat, not ruddy sugar cane."

What Ern doesn't tell Doris is that they don't really have an option. Without the forward payment they can't cover the interest on the machinery loan and the tank loan, or buy seed and fuel to get the next crop into the ground, let alone out again. She makes him a cup of tea and he puts his arms around her middle. She doesn't move or suck herself in; she fills the space perfectly.

The forward-selling merchant is impressive. Within a week he has signed up sixteen of the Wyche district farmers. He visits each place individually in his Hispano Suiza with a tiny golden-coated dog on the front seat. He is from Sydney. He uses a brass slide-rule calculator to assess how much he can pay now and how much on delivery. His checkbook is covered in alligator skin. All sixteen farmers overstate last year's production figures. They see how smoothly the slide rule slides, how easy it is to let it slide a little further.

"In this book I have written proof of my connections in the European market," says the merchant. He pats the book; it too is covered in alligator skin. The farmers nod without asking to inspect it.

The merchant offers fair prices. Prices higher than 1938, when the rain was poor and late, rabbit damage was high, and at least half of the crop had rust.

"Rain, rabbits, and rust. The three *r*'s add up to one big *R*—*Risk*. Forward sell and I carry the risk for you," the merchant spins his spiel. "You can sleep soundly in your bed at night without listening for rain on the roof or for the mice chomping through your crop. It's the modern way of doing business."

The merchant explains that the good prices are the result of his advanced organizational abilities. He books his ships through the Baltic Exchange in London months before the wheat is stripped. The ships are timed to arrive just as the wheat trains chug into the docks. There is no double handling, no risk of demurrage. The wheat is loaded straight from train to ship, the ship turns around and sails back to Europe. The merchant has the seven or eight weeks of the journey to sell. It is this selling afloat that makes him riskier. The other merchants wait until harvest, purchase the product at the best, current market price, sell it out of the country, and then order the ships for its delivery. The offer of some cash now is too much for the Mallee farmers. They don't read the fine print of the contract—the convoluted legalese that allows the merchant to sell at any price once the wheat has left the country and to deduct a massive commission for his efforts.

"Better seven or eight anxious weeks for me than a whole anxious season for you, eh?" the merchant chortles.

"What if you don't sell it?" Ern McKettering asks.

The merchant taps his alligator-skin book. "It's all in here, good sir, every Eye-talian, Frenchie, and Britisher with an interest in Australian Standard White. There's trouble in Europe, Mr. McKettering—even talk of war. You need someone with inside knowledge. It's all here in this book."

Ern signs the contract and follows the merchant out to his car.

"Nice tank you've got there."

"Empty," Ern grunts.

The merchant's dog has moved over behind the steering wheel. It looks up at its master with big limpid eyes.

"Is it a rabbiter?" Ern asks.

"A Pomeranian. A very fine European breed. All the rage in Sydney."

Ern shakes his head. No good for rabbits, too small for stock work. But Doris would love it. Perhaps, he thinks, when the forward-sell money comes in, he'll buy her one.

According to Lola Sprake the merchant had meant to come to us. It was just a matter of timing. He moved through a district in a logical and workmanlike fashion. Only farmers with sufficiently large holdings were approached and only when they were in close proximity to a railway siding. The merchant mapped his movement through the district with a compass and a knack for arriving just as something was coming out of the oven. Our farm happened to be at the end of the line.

The merchant's last morning in Wycheproof, the morning he was coming out to us, started badly. He had hardly slept. A fierce wind had blown the Commercial's sandwich board (STEAK AND KIDNEY PIE WITH PUD. 5/4d) about on the porch below his room for much of the night. He arrived early in the dining room and was attacking a pair of breakfast kidneys when he was disturbed by the muffled sound of Lola's screams. The Pomeranian had bitten her as she stripped the bed. The merchant was forced to leave a slightly larger than normal tip— there was some blood and the need for a sweet sherry. He was glad to be maneuvering his large suitcase down the stairs.

"It's blowy out. You'll be needing your hat," Lola called after him as she wrapped a tea towel around her hand. She knew it was necessary to keep the commercials on side, even ones with questionable personal habits.

The merchant walked up the street to the garage, where the Hispano had been fueled and polished, the dog mincing along behind him. The wind was brisk; he felt it cruelly against his neck. The wind lifted a strip of dust along the railway line dividing the two sides of the main street with a dirty haze. He took a tartan traveling rug from the luggage rack and spread it out on the seat. When the wind died off for a minute he stood against the door letting the weak winter sunshine warm his cheeks. The Hispano fired up nicely. He crossed the railway line and took the Boort Road out of town, double declutching through the gears until he was running smoothly along in top. The Pomeranian sat staring out the passenger window, the wind whipping its lips into a wolfish smile. The merchant was looking forward to signing up the last of the Wycheproof farms, then driving over to Quambatook for a beer and some paperwork before tea.

The paddocks on either side of the road were fallow—a stubbly patchwork of browns and reds. The merchant crossed a culvert at speed, feeling the force of the wind drag at the car for the instant it was in the air. The wind entered the car's gaps and crevices in chilly thrusts. He cursed the fine leather soft top that he had paraded so proudly last summer at Bondi. The dog whimpered and lay down on the seat, folding its head under its belly for warmth. The merchant noticed the sky was pinking up very prettily on the horizon. The wind calmed for a minute and in the sudden quiet he felt a little panicky. He thought about how the car must look from the outside, the sleek black box hurtling through a vast stretch of dead, empty paddock.

The wind buffeted the car again with a jolt and he gripped the wheel hard, relieved to be concentrating on his driving. The solid color of the horizon gave way to a softer, wispier pink. Suddenly the pink cloud was no longer just in front of the car but all around it. The merchant strained into the windshield; it was difficult to make out the road. He turned on the wipers. The blades dragged jerkily in front of his face—they weren't moving rain but a torrent of dirt. He could barely see the road in front of him. God forbid if someone was coming in the other direction. He considered turning around, heading back to town, but the road was terribly narrow and the thought of another evening holed up at the hotel, Mrs. Sprake looking daggers at the dog, convinced him to push on. The map showed the Avoca River wasn't far ahead. He fixed on getting there, taking respite in the trees along the bank and waiting it out.

The dog sneezed and shook its head. The merchant ran his tongue over his teeth; the dirt tasted like iron filings, like old blood. Five miles per hour . . . the speedometer needle rose and fell in small arcs. It was taking forever. The merchant thought of his beautiful Sydney; of warm summers; of cicadas thrumming in his garden; of the saltwater spray over the Harbour Bridge and the smell of frangipani blossoms crushed beneath his tires. His foot grew heavier on the accelerator. Ten miles per hour, twenty, forty . . .

The Hispano hurtled through the dirt, the merchant held the wheel dreamily, loosely. Only when the wooden posts of the bridge were coming up too fast and too close to the passenger side of the car did he snap back into the present with a sudden evasive swerve. Smooth road became rough paddock. The merchant was thrown violently off his seat; the dog became entangled in the gear stick and snapped wildly in alarm and pain. The merchant could just make out the dark shapes of trees in the near distance. He stamped so urgently on the brake his foot slipped off the pedal and caught under the plate.

"Plurry hell. Plurry, plurry hell."

As he cursed, the front wheels of the car hit Robert's new levee bank. It was a perfect takeoff. The bank launched the car acrobatically, gracefully, through the air. A few seconds of silence, then a thunderous splash.

A Hispano Suiza is a luxury car, made well and made heavy; the merchant struggled to release the roof clasps as it sank. The dog, the man, and the tartan rug floated up out of the car into the river. The alligator-skin notebook bumped the merchant's elbow as he performed some rusty breaststroke, then quickly, caught by the current, the notebook took off downstream towards the sea, towards the strange and foreign addresses contained within. The dog was a surprisingly good swimmer for one so short of leg. It made straight for the bank, hauled itself out, and took off across a paddock, its wet tail dragging through the soil like a broom.

No serious injury was done but the car could not be recovered. The merchant was forced to return to Sydney by train and the dog was never seen again.

It was Robert's river control intervention—the levee bank—that prevented the merchant from spinning his spiel at our farm. Robert, who would no doubt have double-tested the dodgy merchant's calculations and insisted on checking the bona fides of the names in the alligator-skin book. Robert, who may have been able to get McKettering and some of the others out of their hastily signed contracts, before it was too late.

RESULTS FROM THE 1939 HARVEST

This year's bushel weight of 45 lbs is once again lower than last year's, confirming a strong and continuing downward trend. The sand drift in the Mallee has devastated grain growing and raises the question whether this area is in fact suitable for any form of cultivation.

In accordance with standard sampling procedure a portion of FAQ (fair–average quality) wheat was critically examined and subjected to analysis and a milling test in the experimental flour mill.

The sample is small and poorly filled out with a dull orange (often due to rust) color. The percentage of screenings is considerably higher than usual, due mainly to a high content of broken grain. The amount of weed seeds (especially thistle) is high as are native grass heads. The moisture and protein content is low.

Purpose: To measure the quality of wheats grown by Mr. R. L. Pettergree of Wycheproof in regard to high yields of good-colored flour with superior baking quality.

Quality Tests: The Pelshenke figure, which indicates gluten quality (time taken for dough ball to expand under water at temperature; time divided by protein content = quality), is average–poor. Mechanical testing of the physical properties of the dough using Brabender's Farinograph and Fermentograph shows poor–average flour quality with acceptable gas-producing power.

LOAF NO.	CRUMB STRUCTURE	CRUST COLOR	LOAF VOLUME	TOTAL
1	5/10	5/10	4/10	14/30
2	4/10	3/10	5/10	12/30
3	6/10	5/10	4/10	15/30
4	4/10	4/10	4/10	12/30
5	5/10	4/10	5/10	14/30
6	5/10	5/10	3/10	13/30
7	4/10	4/10	4/10	12/30
8	4/10	5/10	4/10	13/30
9	1/10	0/10	2/10	3/30
10	4/10	3/10	5/10	12/30

Loaf nine was my error, but the rest are the result of poor flour. These are loaves grown in bedrock and it shows.

Robert was repairing the caravan when I took him the results. He reached inside, placed the piece of paper on the bed, and went back to hammering.

21

SEWING FOR THE FULLER FIGURE

The early morning wind sucks the curtains against the bedroom window. Two flies skitter about on the bedspread. I curl around a pudding bowl sour-mouthed from dry retching. Sister Crock's morning sickness cure was a mixture of gin and honey—the thought of it is enough to make me heave. I roll over and notice the Bible on my night table. A folded flap of paper sticks out:

The word bread *occurs 264 times, wheat 40 times, and* loaves *17 times, according to the standard edition. In the miracle of feeding the multitude of 5,000 people with five loaves and two small fishes, I believe the loaves were unleavened barley cakes—hardly bread. I can't account for the fish.*

I can't account also, for why I have been unable to provide for you in the ways that you want or need. I have work in Wethers.

Robert.

There is a blotch of ink after the word *fish*. He has held the pen too long in thought, allowing the ink to pool and bleed. He often leaves me an article or journal to read, something technical and edifying, but I have never seen him pick up the Bible.

I should be starting on a layette for the baby but first I must finish Doris McKettering's going-away clothes. I sit at Ollie Bowd's sewing machine with a cup of weak black tea and the pudding bowl nearby. The bridge dress is nearly ready. We are having problems with the draped belt inasmuch as it doesn't drape, but encircles her middle. The day dresses need finishing first so Doris can give them a showing here, before they go. The other clothes can wait. I could even post them down, she says, but it would be nice to arrive with everything just so.

The McKetterings' new after-the-farm life will be at the three-story boardinghouse of Ern's aunt at Moonee Ponds. Doris likes the idea of stairs and living layer upon layer, not like here, where everything is so wide and dusty and spread out. Ern and Doris will have the ground floor with the aunt. Above them, four women boarders—shopgirls and typists—and on the top floor four men, two of them "older." I imagine one of the men will have a car and they will all go for drives on the weekend, Doris in the backseat with the shopgirls, Ern in the front smoking a pipe. . . .

The Bible rests on the bodice of Doris's peach satin sundress. Ern could only spare a pound for her new city clothes and the clearing sale didn't bring much, so he was being generous at that. I have cobbled things together, used my samples from the train and unpicked my own clothes for her. The table is a landscape of cloth. Gray linen folds over white lawn over yellow bouclé. Midnight blue satin drips to the floor. Each piece of cloth is pinned to its newspaper pattern. The newspapers are several years old—Ern brought them over after clearing out his shed. I scan each line across to where my scissors have cut through the sentences following Doris's curves:

> Overall poor and disappointing results
> Wheat Crop Championships compet
> H. E. Bath of Donald for *Ghurka*
> weeds, mice, rust, and preventa
> A meeting of the sand drift relief
> the Mallee area. Requests for assis
> The committee reported on the activit
> A bicycle is to be raffled by the Wychepro
> guttering. Although if current drought condi
> be required. Raffle tickets can be purchased at

At the time each of these problems seemed separate and surmountable: drought, mice, sand drift, poor yields. But to read it all together, as the one big picture, it makes us look naive.

The newspapers are thinner these days. The Mallee is emptying out—fewer people, less news. Perhaps we'll be the only ones left—me and Robert and the baby.

The Doris dummy hangs slack-armed on the back of the bedroom door. She's a homemade concoction of brown paper and pillows tied to a coat hanger with string. I miss the modern mannequin from the train with its wind-out bust and hips. I measured Doris thoroughly and tried to classify her figure type as I was taught. When I tied the piece of elastic around her middle and waited for it to roll down to find her natural waist, it stuck fast and I had to cut it free. She has sloping shoulders, a large low bust, full abdomen, and an average seat. According to the chart of special figure types I should avoid empire waistlines, midriff inserts, chemise dresses, and overblouses.

Doris spent her pound on a flat-busk Lady Ruth advertised with a coupon in *Woman's World*. It is designed to coax the abdomen type of figure into more interesting lines and is specially reinforced over the thighs with wide elastic straps. Doris wears the Lady Ruth for fittings. It holds her so firmly her torso feels like a drum. It is only when I measure or pin her arms or the tops of her legs that I can feel the true, warm weight of her.

I imagine her taking tea in the boardinghouse parlor wearing the afternoon dress with interchangeable collars and cuffs; cleaning the grates in the peach satin sundress; carrying breakfast trays up the stairs in the Hungarian cardigan. But mostly I imagine her in the kitchen of the farmhouse, a kaleidoscope of colored biscuit tins like bright wheels above her head. I imagine her looking out the window at the sleep-out where Ern slept as a boy and where, on windy nights, his mother knelt and blew the dust from his eye sockets with her warm breath, and I feel immeasurably sad.

There is only the hemming to finish. Doris is due in the morning to collect her clothes and have a final cup of tea. I sit on a cushion on the back step and sew until the light starts to fade. Then I walk over to the shed and look for some wheat snagged in the hessian of the empty bags. I slide one ear into the hem of each of Doris's dresses and sew a few tiny stitches to keep them in place. Sweet Doris. Let her take the Mallee with her.

* * *

Robert's parting gift to Ern McKettering is a copy of his article from the *Agriculture Journal*: "Everyman's Rules for Scientific Living." It came with a warning. Robert feared for Ern. He considered the practice of scientific living a much more straightforward affair in the country than in the city. At our parting Robert warned Ern that the city's many uncontrollable social factors—politics, fashions, unions, plays—could distract a man from his purpose: "The city, McKettering, is a laboratory. The darndest social laboratory. You'll need your wits about you."

We hugged and kissed them, Doris wept a little, then we waved them good-bye—albeit in a back-to-front sort of way, as Ern's car had a broken gearbox and was stuck in reverse. They drove to the train station, all of ten miles away, backwards. Doris held her vanity mirror on the dashboard for Ern to steer by. The broken gearbox was Ern's last triumph. When the bank manager collected the car from the train station (a final contribution to the McKettering debt) he backed it straight into the bulk silo. The rear end crumpled like paper.

I fetch the journal Robert gave me in the paddock at Jeparit. It is in a drawer of the sewing machine with the thimble and my measuring tape. I lie on the bed and reread the "Rules for Scientific Living" and rub my belly where the skin is sore and stretched.

THE ONLY TRUE FOUNDATION IS A FACT.

This rule makes me think of Sister Crock's lecturette on health and the expectant mother: "At three months of age the human fetus is the size of a large cooking onion. There is a surprising uniformity in the size of the fetus. It appears to remain constant throughout the vastly different physiques and races of the world. The pygmy fetus being of much the same size as the rather tall Norwegian." Or something like that.

AVOID MAWKISH CONSIDERATION
OF HISTORY AND RELIGION.

I think of the days I spent in the soil and cropping wagon helping Robert in the narrow aisle between the plants. How we threw shadows on each other as we worked, watering, measuring, mixing additives, taking notes. When I cut my hands on the wheat Robert took them in his own, examining them intently; then, slipping the canteen from his belt, he dribbled water into my palms; it ran like quicksilver. The heat of his hands surged up my arms and into my body. I felt compelled to say something provocative. Something that would be important to us.

"Robert, do you believe in God?"

"This is my religion, Jean, I believe in this," and he cocked his head to signal everything around us. At that time it was exactly the right answer. "This" was the sun streaming through the glass roof, dazzling us with white light, "this" was the mealy smell of the wheat, the pleasing pattern of the stems swaying against one another in their plots. "This" was surely also me.

KEEP THE MIND FLEXIBLE THROUGH THE
DEVELOPMENT AND TESTING OF NEW HYPOTHESES.

Although Robert's scientific interests are primarily in soils and cropping, he has stretched his mind to other areas. Within the journal is a cutting of an article he had published in the *Graziers' Gazette*:

DEAL LIGHTLY WITH THE LAMB

It is in the best interests of producers that animals intended for export or local trade should arrive at their destination in peak condition. Yet many thousands of carcasses are rejected for export annually due to blemishes, bruises, and wound marks.

With this problem in mind I made an informal study of local graziers and have formed the following hypotheses: much unnecessary knocking about takes place when loading or unloading sheep and lambs or when they are being driven on the hoof. This damage, although not obvious on the live animal, will show up plainly after slaughter.

Dogging, prodding with sticks, whacking, flogging, and lifting by the wool all bring about carcass deterioration.

Livestock buyers are keen to notice any outward signs of damage, due to heavy punishment or knocking about, but are frequently disagreeably surprised to find that they have been deceived by outward appearances. The grazier would do well to deal lightly with the lamb lest he find a heavy loss in his bank balance.

And what of the lamb, Robert? What of its pain and trauma? Is it not enough that we should treat the lamb kindly because kindness is simply good?

BRING SCIENCE INTO THE HOME.

Robert says science brings the potential for infinite human progress, that once the big questions have been solved the scientist will focus in on the small, smaller, smallest things. He predicts the invention of microscopes so powerful they can analyze the very atoms of our being. He says the true attitude of the scientist is to seize hold of things, to permit no ideals or sentimentality but to consider directly, without attachment, each fact he is given.

Four months ago, when I told him about the baby, that was exactly what he did. He took his hat and notebook and went out to examine the *Nabawa* to see how it was standing up to the rust.

22

AT WAR AGAIN

My birthday. Mary sends me a novel and a photograph of her eldest—a sturdy blond toddler who, she says, isn't the least bit shy. Doris sends me a parcel from the city—two crocheted baby's bonnets and some old issues of *Woman's World*. She doesn't say if she's happy at the boardinghouse and she doesn't mention Ern. The magazines are well thumbed and several years old. She recommends the "Modern Mother" pages to me.

GOOD NEWS FOR THE MODERN MOTHER

This is the age of science and wonderful are the things done for poor humanity in its name. The tiny wee brain of a two-month-old baby was penetrated by a tamping pin in a railway yard explosion recently without fatal result. The infant victim remained conscious throughout the harrowing operation that followed and has fully recovered with no ill effects. This astonishing instance of the wonders of modern surgery takes the breath away.

TOILET HINTS FOR THE MODERN MOTHER

If on the too-plump side after your confinement consider a few weeks of reducing but take care not to reduce too quickly. Nature needs time to readjust herself to the new conditions. If you reduce too quickly, flabby muscles will be the unlovely result. Don't encourage a visit from the aging neck—she will surely come to stay.

Robert buys me a crate of oranges and says I must eat them all. The oranges were grown in Mildura. ORANGES. FULL OF GOODNESS FROM THE SUN. EAT MORE ORANGES EVERY DAY IN EVERY WAY, says the sticker on the side of the crate. This would have been enough for me—the waxy sheen of the oranges, some still with a few leaves, a piece of sharp stem attached. The history of the fruit relives as I rub the peel between my hands to release the oil, hold them to my face and inhale. Hello, Dad. But as well as the oranges, which Robert describes as a nutritional supplement, there is an outing—tickets for a rare performance of the Vienna Mozart Boys' Choir to be held in Kerang.

We have been following the travels of the choir, twenty boys on a worldwide tour, recently arrived from New Zealand, in the newspaper. As our new Prime Minister Menzies tours country Victoria, so too, coincidentally, does the choir. While the choir sings to the graziers of Coleraine, Prime Minister Menzies visits a new dairy plant at Warrnambool. As the boys rehearse in St. Arnaud, Mr. Menzies is at a nearby Pomonal merino stud having the delicacies of artificial insemination explained to him so euphemistically he has no idea what he has just heard. The choir and the prime minister shadow each other from town to town.

Mr. Menzies and his entourage of advisors (things are rocky in Europe, instant speeches may be required), and twenty fine Austrian boys, well schooled in their evocations of the Danube, of the snowcapped mountains and great cities of the Fatherland.

The *Ensign* says that the Vienna Mozart Boys' Choir puts the birds to shame. That they are even better than currawongs. We drive to Kerang in convoy with the rest of the Wycheproof contingent. Robert wears his good blue suit and I have sewn some diamond-shaped panels of green cotton into my yellow frock to make it roomier for my expanding waist.

Someone rings a handbell and we find our seats in the hall. A dusty curtain jerks aside to reveal twenty boys in white pompadour wigs and red lipstick. Half of them wear ice blue crinolines; their pale shoulders rise sharply from the low-cut dresses. The other half wear Mozart suits—long jackets, knickerbockers, and tights. There is a crushed and tired look about them—lopsided wigs, a vase of badly bent peacock feathers in the middle of the stage, sagging crinoline hoops. A few seconds' silence, then a soft communal intake of breath. Finally a sound so indescribably pure it seems unlikely it could be coming from the shabby scene in front of us. Some people in the audience actually turn and look over their shoulders to try and locate the true source of the sound. It rolls and grows around us, gaining in force and sweetness. The audience is not so much held still by the sound, but let free. Backs and necks unfurl. Heads reach out, inclined, towards the sound.

They sing Mozart's love opera, *Bastien und Bastienne*. The boys' voices slide together and apart, adding and subtracting with mathematical perfection. I think it is a new way of hearing—not filtering through the ears and brain, but hearing with the body. The baby swoops and jabs inside me as if it is conducting. I would like Robert to take my hand—so I could hear it through his body too.

The next item is *Caccia*—the hunt. The boys mimic the sound of the horns, barking dogs, and the flight of the deer. The conductor is flushed with exertion. I notice Stan Hercules, sitting in the row in front of us, leaning forward in his chair urgently as if he is riding a horse. Then a bizarre rendition of Valtzing Matilda sung in strange, lisping English, as if their mouths are full of bees. It is clear they sing for sound alone, untroubled by the reality of zwagman, villabongs, or yumbuks.

In one corner of the stage a soccer ball rocks slightly. As the boys go offstage they dribble it to the dressing room and then back again. Tricky—to dribble in a crinoline. The program reports that the boys have won many cups for singing and some for soccer. They beat the New Zealand Baptist Boys' team six–nil. They are also keen collectors. One boy has a suitcase full of bath chains and plugs he is planning to take home as keepsakes, and together they save silver paper from all of the chocolates they have eaten on tour. The collection is so large and impressive they hope to sell it on their return to Vienna.

"*Mutti, Mutti,*" chirrups the smallest boy in the final vesper. The mothers of the audience sigh a collective sigh and fold their arms across their chests. To be so far from home, so far from a loving mother to smooth your golden hair.

The applause is uproarious. The conductor, Herr Georg Glebber, a thin man with impressive mutton-chop whiskers, takes center stage to address the audience.

"It is a delight for us to sing for you—noble farmers of Australia. When we sing we give the air a sound. Simple science. We trap the air into a vessel, the body, and let it out again. To travel here today we come through the wheat and oatses. I tell the boys to put their heads out windows and breathe. The air is so thin and so dry it makes in my boys such nice music, yar?"

Glebber bows as we break into applause once again. The concert is called to a close and people file next door to the supper room. Iris has brought Anzac biscuits on our behalf. The boys mingle amongst us, expert at sliding through the crowds to congregate around the supper table. There are vanilla slices toppling sideways from an excess of yellow custard, and lamingtons as thick as house bricks.

Iris looks wistfully at the boys, some still in their white knee stockings and ornately buckled court shoes. "Like little dolls, aren't they, Jean? Wouldn't you like one to take home? Imagine him sitting up on the windowsill warbling away like a bird."

The conductor is standing behind us. Iris turns and smiles at him. He clucks his tongue. "Ah. They look for marzipan, everywhere—Wellington, Auckland, Sydney, they look for marzipan. But no luck!"

We laugh. Iris introduces herself to the conductor and then steers him towards Robert.

"Mr. Glebber, Mr. and Mrs. Pettergree. Mr. Pettergree is our local wheat scientist."

Glebber cocks his head at Robert.

"Ah. So you are the Herr Mendel of Australia. What a life, eh? Peas and celibacy!" Glebber winks at me theatrically. "Do you know in my country Herr Mendel is reaching back into fashion?"

Robert shakes his head.

"He advocated pure breeding to keep constancy of type in the plant. We find that the same is true for the human. Look at my boys, eh, no hybrids, good breeding. All one race—like your wheat, Mr. Pettergree." Glebber reaches out to shake Robert's hand.

"Excuse me, but coffee I must find, something you Australians do not understand at all."

Robert nods at Glebber and watches Iris direct him towards the urn.

"He sounds like Mr. Talbot on sheep breeding. Surely he isn't right?"

"About Mendel or about coffee?"

"Mendel, of course."

Robert frowns. "He's wrong about Mendel but he's right about eugenics. Why would you want to risk defects if you can breed them out?"

I place my hand on my belly. We both turn to look again at the boys around the supper table. They are so handsome and confident, speaking in their guttural German, wishing for marzipan. There was a nervous moment at the beginning of the concert when it looked like they might salute. We waited anxiously for the outstretched Nazi arms but instead they coyly interlaced their fingers and started to swing them from side to side.

"But what about the baby, Robert? We will still love this baby even if it isn't perfect—won't we?"

Before he can answer Iris bustles up and hands me a cup of tea. "I can't stop thinking about Mozart. How he wrote that beautiful music before this country had even been discovered. Imagine that—this whole country just sitting here empty while the rest of the world was listening to opera. How are we ever going to compete with that?" she says.

Stan Hercules joins us. He tells Iris that the whole thing is an unnatural caper—that boys wearing dresses and screeching like girls is against the proper order.

Two of the choirboys dart past us chasing a skink. It hugs the skirting boards, frantically looking for an escape.

Prime Minister Menzies is in Colac when war is declared in Europe. "Australians are a British people," he says, "fitted to face the crisis with cheerful fortitude and confidence," then he returns, quickly, to the city.

The Vienna Mozart Boys' Choir is stuck behind enemy lines. An old army van takes Herr Georg Glebber to the Tatura Internment Camp for Aliens along with many Italians and others with questionable backgrounds. But what of the little vessels—Frederick, Otto, Olaf, Leopold, Gustav, Hans, and the others? It is reported in the papers that they are in limbo. Iris nabs me at the grocer's. She's thinking of taking one, perhaps a small one, but she's worried about the language problem and the difference in "customs." She does feel some sort of responsibility, though, some sort of connection with them since we attended the concert.

Rescue comes from Archbishop Mannix in Melbourne, who sacks his cathedral choir and installs the boys at St. Patrick's. Local families offer to billet them—pleased to help out for a few months.

Robert and I listen to the wireless for two days and two nights on end, but there is little real news. We are at war again. Robert says it will be over quickly—perhaps even before the baby is born.

23

FIRE

Robert and Bill Ivers burn the stubble together. It's neighborly. They do it at night when it's pitch-black outside but the flames light up the house all orange and smoky.

"You're ripening up nicely, love," Bill says when he comes in for a glass of water. His face is covered with soil and trickled with sweat lines. He leaves brown finger marks on the glass.

"Hot out there," he says.

"Hot in here too."

"That'd be right."

"Do you think he'll come in for a drink?" I ask.

Bill brushes a burned wheat stalk off his trouser leg and looks out into the night. "Hard to tell."

They burn at night as the wind is low and the flames won't get away. They light the fires with kerosene tins fitted with a bent pipe and a burning rag at the end. When a rag is extinguished they hold the heads of the lighters together to transfer the flame. I watch them from the back step. They look like puppeteers making two long-necked birds embrace. The fires follow the path left by the harvester in long strips—eating up the scraps. They burn low in some places, high and bright in others as the plant sugars ignite and fizz.

Robert's been out awhile so I pour him a jug of water. I leave my apron hooked over the handle on the back door and duck under the fence. I walk across the dirt towards the burning paddocks. The sky and the land meet in blackness, only the running streams of fire marking one from the other.

I jump over three low lines of fire—choosing the point where it burns lowest. Some of the water spills from the jug and splashes down my thighs. Three fires in front of me now, three behind. I can see Robert just up ahead, holding the lighter. My dress sticks to my legs and I peel it free. I'm looking for the low spot in the next fire, getting ready to jump again, when a sharp pain grips me. A hot metal belt is being tightened around my hips. I drop the jug and bend over the pain. It feels like flesh peeling away. I call out but my voice is lost in the noise of the fires. The pain sharpens. I fall over, kicking with my legs, trying to get out from under it. The jug lies next to my hip, the water drunk instantly by the warm soil.

I am spilling over too—flowing into the soil. Blood seeps from between my legs. I don't know how long I lie like this, then Robert is in front of me and he's saying, "Oh Jesus, oh Jesus," over and over again and picking me up and half dragging and half carrying me. One leg dangles too low through a line of fire and my shoe starts to smolder. Bill runs up with a blanket and smothers it. He tries to drape the blanket over me but it falls. I see it fall in a heap on the soil. I reach my hand out to it. It will be so heavy to wash, I think, I will never get the blood out of it.

Robert slides me onto the backseat of the car, Bill drives. It feels like we are in *Gone With the Wind,* escaping with the glow of the burning ruins behind us. Robert strokes my hair with one hand and holds my shoe with the other.

"Not long now," he says. "Not long now." But his hands are shaking and he's trying not to look at the blood.

Ten days later when I am home from hospital and fed up with bed rest and visits from Elsie, I retrieve the blanket and the jug from the paddock. Some of the fires still smolder but it looks different in the daylight. I try to find the place, the exact place, where I lay and bled.

At six months a stillborn baby is wrapped and disposed of— I don't know where. But I do know that a baby is more than its body, it is fluid too and the meaty surrounds that gave it life. Some of the baby is in the paddock where I lay and bled. I look for a stain—a sign—but it must all have soaked away. In a few months the cultivator will come through. A few more months and the ground will be hidden again under the wheat.

I touch my belly. It is still loose—this cannot be explained by science. Archimedes said when a person gets out of the bath the levels will go back to normal—no more displacement. But not with this. With this, when everything is measured and taken away, nothing will be the same again.

I meet my baby in the night. My dream baby exists in a hazy state as if behind a window painted with glue. I have to strain to make out her features. Dream baby is baby-size, but old. Her neck is lined and she is very thin. She has the face of someone waiting for the end of life, not the beginning. But as I struggle to make out her features I think, each night, she is getting a little younger. I think that if she were back inside me again her liquid gestation in the waters of my body would grow her young again, make her plump and fresh and new. Except that this would be in ideal conditions, not in the conditions of the Mallee.

I write to Mary about the baby. Although it is hard to find the words. There is just the born and the unborn. There are no words for someone caught in between. She came too soon, I say. There was something of the monkey about her. She was so soft. The flesh of her arm melted under my touch like butter. She was both too young and too old. Her chin was sharply pointed. She was too tired to open her tiny eyes to me. For the first time in my life I wanted my mother.

I draw Mary a map of the paddocks around the house. I mark the place that I fell in early labor and the place where Folly was set alight near the river. I tell Mary that Robert is in great pain about the baby. I can see that this is true although he cannot talk to me or even hold me for fear, I think, of being overwhelmed. I wish Mary love and happiness. I say that I'm sure she can talk her George around and put paid to his ridiculous ideas about going to the war.

RESULTS FROM THE 1940 HARVEST

The sample size is smaller as some farmers have switched to flax due to wartime demand. This year's bushel weight of 44 lbs is low. Although economic factors have improved, environmental ones have not.

In accordance with standard sampling procedure a portion of FAQ (fair–average quality) wheat was critically examined and subjected to analysis and a milling test in the experimental flour mill.

The sample is heavily rust-infected and shows evidence of bunt and stinking smut. The grains are small but of a constant size. Their appearance is not unpleasing.

The percentage of native grass seeds is high. Moisture content and protein content are low.

Purpose: To measure the quality of wheats grown by Mr. R. L. Pettergree of Wycheproof in regard to high yields of good-colored flour with superior baking quality.

Quality Tests: The Pelshenke figure, which indicates gluten quality (time taken for dough ball to expand under water at temperature; time divided by protein content = quality), is below that which can be recorded. Mechanical testing of the physical properties of the dough using Brabender's Farinograph and Fermentograph shows extremely poor flour quality with little gas-producing power.

LOAF NO.	CRUMB STRUCTURE	CRUST COLOR	LOAF VOLUME	TOTAL
1	3/10	3/10	4/10	10/30
2	2/10	3/10	4/10	9/30
3	2/10	2/10	3/10	7/30
4	2/10	3/10	2/10	7/30
5	3/10	3/10	1/10	7/30
6	2/10	2/10	2/10	6/30
7	0/10	0/10	0/10	0/30
8				
9				
10				

24

THE ONE-IN, ALL-IN TRAIN BRINGS
WAR TO THE MAN-ON-THE-LAND

An advertisement on the front page of the *Ensign* catches our
attention:

The One-In, All-In Train will stop at Wycheproof on 14th and
15th May 1940. Take a few minutes out from your busy sched-
ule to view the impressive displays. See modern weapons of war:

1 Tank. Light. Mark VI
1 4 Wheel Drive Ford V8 with guns
1 Clectrac with medium artillery
1 Trench Mortar
2 Flamethrowers
1 Field Gun

Also many large-scale models depicting the new scientific
warhorses of the RAAF, AIF, and Navy and special displays for
women from the Australian Defence League.

All men aged 18–35 are encouraged to attend. Men of the

country—Australia Calls—will YOU answer? Are you going to wait till Nazi tanks roll up Australian beaches or Axis planes smash your mother's home? Don't deceive yourself—you'll be too late then. The War is rushing closer to Australia every day. Go out to meet it now!

On the afternoon of the 15th the Matron-in-Chief will conduct the preliminary medical examination of local enlistees in Car 2.

In the same issue of the *Ensign* there is a reprinted article on the military might and sophistication of the New Zealand Army. According to the article, for the first time ever an army is giving consideration to the mental capacity of its recruits. Men who front to enlist are given a comprehensive intelligence test. Only then are they spread across different units of the army to provide the best possible mix of intelligence and strength.

After reading the article and drinking several cups of tea in silence, Robert starts a fresh page in his notebook. He calculates the strength of the New Zealand Army based on the exact numbers of Class I, II, and III recruits. He says with this information it should be possible to capture the war as an equation. Except there is a lot of supposing about the strength and intelligence of the Axis and even about the Allies.

Can we assume a Frenchman, a Brit, or an Aussie will have the same brains as a New Zealander? It all seems irrelevant to me. Each of them will have the same capacity for death. But as he sits hunched over his calculations I am relieved that he's doing something, that he's been released for a while from the frozen state. No agriculture is under way on the farm—neither scientific nor plain everyday. The fences are falling into disrepair. Since the last baking test Robert has divided his time between the caravan and the house. Some days he heads off on the tractor with the caravan hitched behind, others he slouches around from room to room, returning eventually to the kitchen.

I walk to the river each morning. I like the quiet of the farm without the machines at work. The crop has started to push through of its own accord. Wheat seed that has lain dormant from the past is threaded with the native wallaby grass Robert so derided on the train. I wonder how many of the tiny heads I would need to collect to bake a loaf? And what it would taste of, the true bread of ancient Australia? If I am walking barefoot I pick out the silvery stems to stand on—they are much softer than the sharp wheat stems, like lengths of strong cotton. When I retrace my steps on my way back, the crushed stems have already risen again, as if I had never been through.

Sometimes when I return to the house Robert has done some work that was rightly mine—swept the floors or washed the tea towels and hung them in precise formation on the line. I feel as if I am returning to a ship with her flags flying the alert.

On May 14 we go into town to see the train. Most of the district goes—but of course we have a special interest. It is the same engine, K109, rescued from the rust yards at Essendon. Still a dusty burnt orange. The sign on the engine's nose has been painted over but the faint shadow of BETTER-FARMING TRAIN can still be seen behind the new lettering. The One-In, All-In Train is shorter—only three carriages and a wagon.

We stand back for a minute, taking the scene in, when a

door in the middle carriage opens and Mr. Plattfuss lowers himself down. His mustache has faded and he's put on a bit of weight but it is unmistakably him. He wears the familiar white dust coat over his shirtsleeves and an army tie. He reaches back into the carriage, drags out several rolls of canvas, and hoists them onto his shoulder. Robert squeezes my arm and walks over to help him. I watch Mr. Plattfuss turn as Robert says his name, and the look of surprise and recognition on his face. They shake hands warmly, then Robert helps him tie three canvas banners along the length of the train.

False teeth or defective teeth are no bar to
enlisting in the AIF.
The Army will look after your teeth.

By the way, how's your chest measurement?
If it is 32 inches or more, put an AIF tunic
around it.
You are wanted urgently!

Army recruits invariably put on weight.
Join the AIF and carry more weight for your
country!

Mr. Plattfuss hoists himself back into the train and Robert follows. I expect Mr. Plattfuss will ask Robert about Folly and I wonder what he will say: That the experiment was a failure; that science can't tame the Mallee; that we couldn't even keep the old scrub cow alive?

I walk down to my carriage. The women's carriage. The stationmaster's collie lies in the sun by the door. I bend down and rub his ears and drag my fingers through some of the matted fur around his neck. He blinks and swallows in appreciation. If Mary were here she would have been sneaking treats to him. The door opens behind me and I hear the steps being lowered.

"We're open now. Feel free to come in for a look."

The familiar voice of Sister Crock. I stand up and turn around. She looks so bright and round framed in the carriage doorway. Her starched white dress is tight across the hips. Her red felt midi cape sits askew on her ample shoulders. She squints out at me, then her fingers fly to her lips in surprise.

"Miss Finnegan! Sorry—Mrs. Pettergree, rather! Well, I didn't expect to see you here. We thought you'd long gone from the Mallee. Come and have some tea, dear, and tell me all your news."

It is impossible not to smile at her. Or to resist her bustling me over to sit on the front pew while she makes tea at the baby-weighing table with a new electric kettle. Mary's oven still stands in the corner along with my blackboard, the same white paint peeling from the frame. My dressmaking mannequins are kitted out in AIF winter greens with slouch hats pushed low on their blunt necks. The shelves where we displayed the jams and bottled fruits are now fronted with placards. BE PROUD OF HIM IN THIS, one says, referring to the uniform below.

> Girlfriends, mothers, sisters and wives, imagine
> how proud you'll feel of him in uniform! You'll
> be able to say with a lifted chin, "My boy's with

the AIF." Encourage him to join up today and
get the finest job a man can have.

Sister Crock taps the aluminum teapot with a spoon to settle
the tea leaves.

"We thought you'd up and gone, dear. There's not many still
left out here."

"We're hanging on. My husband doesn't give in easily. Or
perhaps it's more that he's not sure what to do next."

"Yes, I remember that about your husband. A certain deter-
mined nature. Now I suppose you've heard all about Mary's
brood but what about you? Any children?"

I look at the floor. "No. I lost a baby last year. It was difficult,
with the drought. . . ."

Sister Crock smiles at me sympathetically and takes a sip
from her tea. "It isn't easy on women. Mr. Plattfuss says it is the
same for horses. When it's too dry they can't carry all of the way.
Drought foals, he calls them."

There is a long pause. I pick up a pamphlet from the table.
The words are blurry. It is addressed to women. Women like me.

WOMEN OF AUSTRALIA—WHAT YOU CAN DO TO HELP

1. *Promote a defense conscience in the home*
2. *Organize and attend lectures on patriotic subjects*
3. *Instil love of Country and Empire in your children*

Sister Crock places her teacup on the table. "Don't let me
forget, I have some letters for you."

"For me?"

"Yes. From Mr. Ohno. When the train disbanded he went to work at a big poultry factory in Drouin. Then last year I heard he'd been taken away to a prison camp for aliens. It's at Tatura, some awful place they put all the men from the wrong countries to stop them from spying. It's a loss to chicken sexing but I suppose the government knows best. He sent the letters to Wycheproof but they were all returned—'not at this address.' Isn't that funny? He hadn't put the camp's address on the outside of the envelope—Japanese pride, I suppose—but there was a sketch of the Better-Farming Train on the back of one of them so the post office sent them to me. I opened a few—just a few—to see if there was anything I could assist with. Very odd. He seems to think you may have died. 'Out there in the red sand,' he says, 'you may have died.'"

She pours me a second cup of tea and tells me to have a look around while she fetches the letters from her sleeping compartment.

Robert invites Mr. Plattfuss home for tea. I have nothing to give him except crackers and jam but he's polite about it. Says he's sick of heavy food and he's heading for a counter tea afterwards at the Commercial, where he is giving a recruiting talk about the AIF and showing some lantern slides on the wall. Then he's to put three pounds on the bar to get the drinking and talking started.

"Oiling the camaraderie," he calls it. Robert offers to drive him in and help him set up the equipment.

Mr. Plattfuss says he misses the old days on the farming train. He especially misses his cows. As he stands to leave he crushes me to him in a hug and says, "I'm so sorry, my dear, I'm so very sorry."

I'm not sure if he's talking about Folly, or if Sister Crock has told him about the baby, or if it's just about Robert and me and the farm.

I wave them good-bye from the step, Mr. Plattfuss stroking his mustache and doing some vocal exercises to prepare himself for public speaking, Robert purposeful at the steering wheel, happy to be caught up in something again.

25

MR. OHNO'S LETTERS

Mr. Ohno's letters are tiny. They fit perfectly into their miniature envelopes of folded paper with no gum or glue. "Not at this
address" is scrawled on the front of each envelope in Robert's
handwriting.

I open the first envelope, releasing the hand-pressed notches
and tabs. I half expect one of Mr. Ohno's paper cranes to un-
bend itself from flatness and fly out, or perhaps another erotic
postcard, but in each envelope there is just one small letter. The
writing starts in English but then moves into Japanese script.
Some of the letters and envelopes have a tiny drawing: a cup, a
shoe, a tree with long weeping leaves.

Deer Mrs. Jean,
  *Each rising sun I think you. Mrs. Jean face like litl nut. I think
you when galas walk on the rowd. I can nevr stopping. I for always
you. Sad for you, sad for snow. Help me. Mrs. Jean in the sand.*
  Ples send dodoes and bells.

                                                          Ohno

Deer Mrs. Jean,

I make hats for army men. My fingrs are short now. No good for chikens. I think about you in the sand. Why you get of in the sand? Mrs. Jean with hairs so sof. Are you died in the sand? Help me Mrs. Jean. I am not dangerows to this cuntry. I for always you Mrs. Jean. Ples send dodoes and bells.

Ohno

Deer Mrs. Jean,

You nevr make writing with me? I am so sad. I have now man who makes sounds. Mr. Glebber from Austria a singing teacher. Like you Mrs. Jean? He make for me a shamisen from fruit box. I ask him to make writing for me. Ples send dodoes and bells.

Ohno

Then a longer letter in an ordinary, cheap gray envelope.

Internment Camp 1 Tatura, Victoria the Southeast of Australia
Dear Mrs. Jean,

Mr. Ohno, a fellow prisoner and Asiatic, has asked me to write to you. He is friendless here (excepting myself). He speaks English quite passably (he is saying he is a professor of chickens) but his composition is poor. Mr. Ohno is convinced that you are able to assist him in some way. He tells me that you met on a train? and asks you make a composition to the government to request his release. He says he is only here because of the chickens and that he has no interest in politics or war. I play chess with him every day and we make hats for the soldiers. On the weekends we play golf with the Italians.

Mr. Ohno asked me to send you this drawing. He says it is a blessing for Hari-Kuyo—an Asiatic concert for broken needles. The monks sing a special mass for all of the needles broken during the year. The unfortunate needles are placed in a cake of Tovu (I think he means icing?) so they have a safe place to rest. This will soothe them after their days of hard service. Mr. Ohno wishes me to say that the needle must be taken care of. In the hands of a skilled dressmaker a needle can fly. He says you are a needle of great strength and harmony.

I hope this is not offensive and that it makes sense to you. Finally, Mr. Ohno asks you to please send photographs and news.

I am saying a little of my situation as well, which is dire. I am the Conductor of the world-famous Vienna Mozart Boys' Choir, which due to world events, has been caught on this enemy island. My boys are in good care in Melbourne but I am stuck in this wasteland. It is an appalling venue. Frozen cold in winter and even more terrible in summer—droughts, dust storms, brain-boiling heat, and swarms of poisonous black bumblebees. There is no coffee and I am having to wear ill-cut clothes. I have set up a choir amongst the men. The Italian prisoners can harmonize, but the guards are of poor type.

I request you to send the following:

1. *Three large books of musical notation paper (5-line stave).*
2. *A winding phonograph with all Mozart recordings available to you.*
3. *Any mass or sacred music by Gluck, Salieri, Haydn, or Schubert set for a men's choir.*
4. *A necktie.*
5. *Marzipan.*

> *With Appreciation,*
> *Herr Georg Glebber,*
> *Conductor-in-Exile*

I read and reread the letters through the night. Always listening for the car, always ready to put them away, but Robert doesn't come home. At dawn I fold them in a scrap of satin from one of Doris's dresses and put them in a drawer of the sewing machine and try to sleep.

26

AT THE COMMERCIAL

Lola Sprake makes Robert a rum and cloves. He was never big on liquor, has hardly been into the bar these past years. A man without much value, in Lola's opinion—neither a drinker nor busy with his pockets. Mr. Plattfuss offers Lola a Ladies' Beer for helping him to remove the dartboard but she doesn't drink while working, except for a cordial to wet the lips.

All the usual suspects are in, as well as a few just for the talk. Some older men—veterans, in their Sunday suits—pull a couple of tables together and sit in their own private cloud of smoke and talk near the door. Stan Hercules is propped at the bar with his camera and notebook laid out in front of him. This is the closest a small-town newspaperman will ever get to being a war correspondent and he's relishing it. Mr. Plattfuss takes his position by the projector. Hercules taps his glass with a pencil: "Quieten up there, men, the show's about to start."

Mr. Plattfuss takes a swig from his Ballarat Bitter and clears his throat. He switches on the projector and a wedge of yellow light shines on the side wall. He takes a piece of paper from his pocket and starts to read: "This nation of three million square miles contains approximately seven million people. There is no doubt that each of those seven million Australians loves their country."

"Hear, hear," the bar responds in unison. A few men stamp their feet and whistle.

Mr. Plattfuss continues: "If this country is good enough to have, it is good enough to hold. To hold it we need defense. But it is a weak excuse indeed for an eligible man to say he will stay here and defend us rather than sign up. One look at all the devastation and destruction in England will show the calamitous absurdity of such a thought.

"Since Nazism first commenced its assault on civilization, Australia has devoted many millions of pounds to the building of war material and munitions. We hear the word *sacrifice* when people talk of this war. Is it a sacrifice or is it a privilege to share in the service of one's country, a country in which personal freedom is given the greatest possible latitude?"

Mr. Plattfuss takes a deep swig of his bitter. The men watch as he replaces the glass neatly on its beer mat and turns back to his notes.

"I hear you ask, what will *you* get out of this war? Well, the modern soldier is a man of science. The days of hewing away with a sword or bayonet through the ranks of the enemy are gone. This war will be won by machines. By men who can match their pluck with their skill.

"The army will give you expensive, valuable training for free. Each unit requires specialized knowledge, which can only be obtained through a rigorous course of scientific study. Am I the right man for this skillful work? I hear you ask. Yes, is the reply. If you can drive a car you can maneuver a tank, if you can sail a boat you can command a battleship, if you can fly a kite you can belly-roll a bomber."

The men cheer. Mr. Plattfuss waits until the noise dies down before continuing.

"The Forces will take you away from dull routine to life in the open air, association with clean-living, disciplined, and fit young men in a fellowship of immortal comradeship. I ask all of the men here tonight, whatever your age and fitness, to visit the One-In, All-In Train tomorrow and think seriously about your future. Thank you and good evening."

Mr. Plattfuss downs the rest of his bitter during the applause and is quickly presented with another. The men ask to see the slides again and he flicks backwards and forwards, leaving the last slide—an aerial torpedo—shimmering on the wall of the pub.

Robert has three more rum and cloves and then some beer from the jug of a man he doesn't know. He listens to Mr. Plattfuss complain about the selling off of his prize cows and the difficulties of working with people rather than animals.

It's getting late, the pub talk is getting louder. Men loosen or remove their ties, they slouch at the bar or sit back to front on chairs or lean on one another. There are hoots and cheers as bets and contests are won and lost. They challenge one another to scull a pot or roll a beer mat farthest along the floor. Mr. Plattfuss is no longer around but Robert doesn't remember him leaving. The man who keeps filling Robert's glass looks familiar although Robert can't quite place him. He is unused to so much beer—he is full up with liquid, sloshing about in himself.

"Do I know you?" he asks the plain-looking man, and waits, head cocked, mouth open, for the reply.

"You could say so, Mr. Pettergree. You could say you know me." The man looks tired, worn out before his time. He grimaces, seems to be deciding something.

"I'm just another mug farmer, that's me. You must know a truckload of 'em."

Robert thinks about this for a minute. "Is it something to do with me? Have I misled you at some time?" he asks, but he slurs his words and the *misled* comes out as *missiled*, which makes him laugh.

The man's anger rises suddenly. He spits at Robert, "Funny? You think it's funny? You humiliate me in front of everyone, you cause me to lose my crop, my mortgage, my insurance, and you think it's funny?" The man rubs the knuckles on his right hand. "Strewth, who do you think you are, Pettergree, the bloody oracle?"

Robert shifts in his seat. "Ah, I think I can place you. . . . Les . . . red land at Towaninnie. Les Noy. My wife said you'd been to visit. I think it was a while ago. . . ." Robert trails off, trying to think exactly what Noy had brought and if he should be thanked.

Noy's face is reddening and getting blotchy with it. "Outside."

"Sorry?"

"Outside, man, now." He kicks out at the bar stool as he stands. It looks more childish than menacing.

Robert scans the bar for a familiar face. Most of the older men have left. He wishes that Ern McKettering were there, leaning against the wall in his white cricket boots. He stands unsteadily and heads for the door. Noy has twisted the shoulder of his jacket into a tight handle. He pushes Robert firmly from behind. It looks almost friendly to anyone watching—anyone not sober, that is. Robert is marched through the front door, along the footpath, and around the back of the hotel. A fire flickers in a forty-four-gallon drum amongst the outhouses and stacks of empty beer barrels and rubbish bins. A small group of men stands around the drum drinking from bottles in brown paper bags. Noy shoves Robert towards the stack of barrels.

"You're cockeyed, man. You go around doling out advice—do this, do that—and it's just stuff you've read in books, for chrissakes. Let me tell you, Pettergree, anyone can read a book, a bloody nipper can read a book. Where's your bloody experience?"

Noy advances on Robert and jabs him in the chest as he speaks. Robert pushes his hand aside—not out of anger. Just to stop him touching his ribs. The drink has changed Robert's center of balance; his head feels so light, barely there—all of him seems to be lined up behind his sharp sternum. Noy is circling him with his fists up, waiting for something, a defense or the first jab.

Robert forces himself to think. "Did you plant the superior variety, Mr. Noy?" He's aware of how ridiculous this sounds and how the circle of men around the fire has dissolved and formed again—around him and Noy. "Did you use the right additives?"

"Strewth." Noy swings a punch at Robert's head but it just misses. "Come on, put 'em up, put 'em up. You're not a farmer's bootlace, Pettergree. You're not a farmer's fucking backside."

Robert crosses his arms over his chest. He loses his balance and stumbles sideways onto an empty barrel. His voice is barely more than a whisper. "Do you have a wife, Mr. Noy? I think . . .

a man as a single unit of production . . . it isn't viable." Tears wash across his face. His voice is caught somewhere deep in his throat. "A wife. To provide for a wife is essential. . . ."

Noy slaps his fists against his sides in frustration. You can't hit a man when he's down, especially not if he's down *and* crying like a child. The circle of men shuffles back a few steps—it's over. Noy feels strangely responsible for Robert. He brought him out here and now he's slumped in the dirt with his head in his hands making everyone uncomfortable.

"Get up. Come on, get up."

Robert doesn't move. Noy tries to pull him up by his collar but he's a dead weight.

A dark-haired man with a pretty pair of false teeth steps forward. "Leave it, mate. You'll rip his bloody clothes off."

The man introduces himself to Les Noy as Neville Frogley, a laborer who likes a spot of fishing and who did some work here a while back during the sand drift. Frogley drags Robert to his feet and holds him steady under the arms.

"You see, young Leslie, there's better things can be done with 'im. He's a regular Mr. Magic, he is. We'll be making a quid or two out of him tonight. Our Mr. Pettergree has a special talent, and as we know, it's not for the growin' of wheat."

Robert tries to protest. He tells them that he doesn't do the tasting anymore. That he only did it for Lillian, his mother, who had things hard in the old country, that's he's dedicated his life to science. . . . But the men just laugh and drag him farther off into the darkness.

27

A NIGHT OF SOIL

Neville Frogley props Robert up on a sugar-gum stump on the outskirts of town. Les Noy keeps the beer coming. They charge a pound a bet. It crosses Frogley's mind that advanced drunkenness may reduce Robert's ability. It doesn't.

Robert tastes white soil from the shores of Lake Tyrrell, black soil from Horsham, red soil from Wycheproof, soil laced with pepper (stating correctly that it is white pepper, not black), soil mixed with kalsomine, soil moistened with kerosene, soil mixed with shit.

He can barely hold himself up. Neville Frogley feeds the soil through Robert's lips with his fingers, then leans in to catch the slurry, mumbled verdict.

Robert's mind flicks backwards—his mother's red hair, Uncle Will and his pigeons, years of lonely evenings in the library, the honey car, starting the tractor on a cold morning, the first harvest, Jean watering the houseplants in her cotton slip, Jean pale and weak in hospital asking him to open the curtains and let in the Mallee sky. . . .

He is aware enough to recognize some of the men that stand around him. He is aware enough to see his humiliation clearly. A scientist—a failed scientist—performing tricks like a circus freak. There is no going back, he thinks to himself. There is no way to recover from this.

Neville Frogley makes six pounds, four shillings, and three-pence. He gives Les Noy half and disappears just as the magpies start warbling and the first light is spreading softly through the trees.

Noy waves the money in front of Robert. "How much do you want, then, mate—for services rendered?" Robert stares into his face for a second, then splatters vomit across his shoes.

Noy looks around at the remains of the fire and the empty beer bottles and Robert slumped sideways on the tree stump. "Strewth. Why do I always get left holding the baby?"

Robert comes home not long after dawn. I hear him opening and closing the drawers on the sewing machine. I pull the coverlet around me and go to see what he's up to.

"Where's the tape measure?"

He looks rough. His suit is crumpled and dusty, as if he's been out in a soil storm. He takes off the coat and then his shirt. The white cotton is flecked with fine red soil, giving it a rosy hue.

"The tape measure?"

"Bottom drawer." I know what he's doing. The minimum AIF chest measurement is thirty-two inches with two inches for expansion. A pigeon chest distorts the chest but it doesn't in-crease it. The outward swell at the sternum is more than offset by the flattening of the ribs. Front-on it might not be noticeable, but the tape measure doesn't lie.

He struggles to get the tape around his back.

"Can you help me?"

I take the two ends and slide it up—across his nipples. He smells of beer and soil and vomit. My hands brush his upper arms where the firm muscle puckers and folds into the softness of his armpits.

"It isn't going to work. It's just thirty, and barely that."

"Maybe they'll have a different tape?"

"Last time I heard there is only *one* way of measuring."

Robert twists to pull his shirt back over his shoulders. "I can't see why it matters so much. I'm as fit as the next man."

"Perhaps you need a certain width for a decent target. Perhaps it's an international rule of war and the Huns have the same requirement. Just to make it fair, of course."

"You're being ridiculous, Jean."

"No. I'm being honest."

We both look down. All of the drawers on the sewing machine cabinet are open. Robert stands dully, tired. Then he breathes in sharply through his mouth, leans down, and takes the little parcel of letters from the second drawer. He holds them in the palm of his hand and sorts through them with slow concentration, as though looking for something misfiled.

"Who gave you these?"

I snatch the letters off him and hold them in front of me.

"I saw your handwriting on the envelopes. I'm the one that should be angry here."

"I didn't read them," he says casually.

"You lied to me. You prevented me from helping a friend. Ohno has been sent to prison, Robert, and he has nobody."

He starts to do up his buttons. His mouth is held tight with pride but his face is hurt and loose around it.

"Your heart was always elsewhere."

"My heart? My heart? How can you talk about my heart?" I put the heels of my hands on his chest and push him backwards. His thigh catches on the edge of the sewing machine. He winces and rubs at it. He looks surprised. Confused.

"My heart has always been here for you. Everything was about love—can't you see that? Every experiment, every sample, every hopeless loaf of bread, it was all about love, Robert. My love for you. And what did you give me? Useless rules. Where is the heart in your useless rules? The rules don't mean anything, Robert. They just get in the way of you seeing things how they really are. They get in the way of the truth."

The sun is rising. It streams in through the open kitchen door, refracting a long blade of light across the floor between us. We stare at each other across the kitchen, across the blade of light. Robert seems tired and weak. Exhausted. One of his shoulders droops low, his arm hanging slackly from it so he seems to be listing or struggling against a head wind. I take his slack arm, walk him to the door, and stand behind him. The sunlight is bright and glittery and he puts out his hand to shade his eyes.

"What do you see, Robert? Tell me what you see."

We stand in silence for a minute. I put my arms around him from behind and knot my fingers together across his chest. His back blots out my view but I can smell the day as it starts to unfold. The aroma of the soil baking on a low, strong heat, the dry wheat, the nose-twitching sting of the peppercorn tree. I lean on Robert and nudge him forward. I want us to move out from the frame of the door into the picture together. He shakes his head. Then he unlaces my fingers from across his chest and shrugs me off.

"Robert?" I reach out to him again, try to hold him to me. I want him to feel my body through my clothes. I want to push against him so that there are no spaces between us, just layers of skin and flesh and muscle and bone. I want him to feel me as I am.

I hear him swallow and feel him hardening through his trousers, but then he pushes me aside and lurches through the door.

"It's too late, Jean. It's too late now."

28

SISTER CROCK PROCLAIMS THE MEN FIT

Hec Bowd isn't at the Commercial but he can't ignore what's happening. He reads the paper, hears the bugle calls, sees the Clectrac tank roll heavily down the main street. It's a close relation to the special sand tractor that went to his neighbor when he was sold up. That was war too. The battle of the shifting soil. No one, it turns out, was the victor—not even the bank.

The Bowds left the farm for a "Florida villa" on the edge of town. It was a constant cruel reminder—the dado design of it with kero tins below and flapping wheat sacks above. Mrs. Bowd never came around to it. She took to her cot and passed away soon after. Hec and Ollie are the survivors. They keep to themselves. He takes the odd harvest job and Ollie does a bit of baby-sitting. Ollie has to wear her tennis whites every day and she finds it hard to keep them clean.

When the recruiting train comes through Hec says they'll just go down for a look. A quick stroll to the station—catch up with some old faces. But on the way, his daughter's arm folded gently through his, he knows what he has to do. The bugle calls in the distance as they cross the river. Hec is as jumpy as a kitten. How can he leave his girl? Lovely Ollie with her sharp chin and gleaming dark eyes. But how else to put five bob a day in her purse? And the pension is good. If he comes back injured (he thinks this is unlikely) she'll be well looked after, and if he is killed (most likely) she'll get the same as the widow's pension—a bit of money and some dignity with it.

At forty-five Hec's way too old to fight, but his papers went with the mice and who's going to argue? It's his teeth he worries about. He's had them thirty-odd years and they seem to be getting bigger and more uncomfortable as the years go by. He has to take them out to eat. In fact he takes them out most times except for church and odd evenings down the pub and Ollie's birthday. It takes him several minutes to coax the teeth into place and they often loosen and crash about in his mouth if he runs. He can't imagine fighting in them.

A man of forty-five may look thirty-five if he's a soft-handed city fellow who has spent his days riding a desk—slinging ink. But not a farmer. Every one of Hec Bowd's years on the farm is written across his face. Thickened blotchy skin, a scorch mark across the forehead from the band of his hat, eyes of faded china blue.

Sister Crock has made a smooth transition from measuring babies to measuring men. She is happy to bend the rules for her country. Sister Crock accepts—she rarely rejects. Why send only the perfectly fit to get killed? she reasons. Why not give everyone a chance? She is creative. With a stroke of her pen a wizened man of fifty stumbling over his date of birth has it recorded, in neat nurse's handwriting, as 1910, making him exactly thirty.

She is helpful, too, with occupations. "Far too many occupations are classified," she complains to Mr. Plattfuss. When a man is told he will not be accepted if he describes himself as a farmer, Sister Crock assists him in adopting another occupation. Her father worked all of his life in the leather-tanning industry, so the farmers of the Mallee became shed men, hand fleshers, buffing machinists, vat hands, unhairers, paddle hands, lime jobbers, strikers, and squeezing machinists. And sometimes, for a man of a different class, she said he was a clock maker. She went out with a clock maker for a few months during her training and occasionally wondered how her life might have been different if they'd made a go of it.

Hec Bowd leaves Ollie to look at the displays in the women's car and says he'll pick her up later—when he's seen some mates and had a beer or two. He's third in line at the enlistment card table. A young man from the recruiting office takes his details, asks a few questions (can you drive a car, cook, use a typewriter, take shorthand, keep accounts, or play a musical instrument?) and sends him down the line to the sister. He'd been hoping for a doctor. The short-arm inspection isn't something to be relished in front of a woman.

The examination car is partitioned off into several stalls with green cotton curtains. Each stall contains a chair. Sister Crock, busy with somebody in stall three, calls out for Hec to take a vacant stall and undress. Hec leans heavily against the chair. His shoes are laced with baling twine. He takes them off and lays his trousers on top of them. He sits on the cold, hard chair and waits.

"Next man, come through now."

Hec plucks at the edge of the curtain. On the other side of it Sister Crock sits behind a sizable leather-topped desk flanked by a set of scales and a measuring stick. She reads out a series of questions without even looking up at him.

"Have you had a broken nose or a serious injury? Have you been operated on? Has any member of your family suffered from pleurisy, tuberculosis, diabetes, stroke, nervous breakdown, or mental trouble? Have you ever been rejected for life insurance?"

"Er, no. Not that I can think of."

She writes something on a white card and finally looks up at him.

"Mr. Bowd." Her eyes travel from his face down to the floor.

Hec can feel himself shriveling. His cock is pointing to the left, caught up in the wiry nest of his pubic hair. He wishes he'd thought to free things up down there before coming through the curtain.

"Not exactly in the flower of your youth, are you, Mr. Bowd?"

Hec holds his tongue. She's no spring chicken herself and he would have liked to tell her so, but he doesn't want to expose his dentures with any smart speech.

"Stand against the measure, please. Heels touching."

Sister Crock brings the adjustable rule down until it rests on Hec's smooth skull. He wishes for his hat.

"Five-seven." She weighs him and measures his chest. "Have you ever worn eyeglasses, Mr. Bowd?"

"No. Not that I can think of."

Hec holds a well-thumbed cardboard square over each eye and reads the test chart.

"F N P O H V D L X."

It's a good job, an optometrist, he thinks. Maybe Ollie could get a job in an optometrist's office and spend her days polishing lenses and making appointments. She'd have to move to the city—Horsham, or Bendigo even.

Sister Crock writes "20/20" under Vision and moves on to General Physique and Configuration.

"Turn around, Mr. Bowd." She assesses Hec's rear view for scoliosis, varicose veins, and hemorrhoids. She makes him turn to the front again, stand on his toes, stand on his heels, squat, swing his arms around, bend his elbows, open and shut his hands, pronate and supinate one forearm. Then, bending forward, she examines him for disabilities of the mouth ("dentures present but no deformities of the jaw noted"), throat, and ears; for hernia and for scrotal abnormalities. She stands and examines his heart and lungs with a stethoscope. The final test is hearing. She advises him to occlude one ear ("It means 'cover,' Mr. Bowd") and walks to the rear of the carriage where she whispers a few numbers for him to repeat. "Sixty-six," she whispers. "Twenty-five, forty-four." She makes allowances for men in cropping areas—long hours on noisy tractors take their toll. The whisper rises to a bark.

Sister Crock stamps Hec's card and passes him his AA A204. Private Hector Bowd has a week to tidy up his affairs and present himself in Melbourne. He pulls his trousers on with difficulty. He's shaking and not sure whether it's from fear or relief. Now for the hard bit. To find Ollie and break the news.

* * *

Sister Crock doesn't reject men for showing evidence of inebria-
tion. She's aware of the three pounds on the bar, of the hours of
drinking a man may need to put in the night before to get himself here. She doesn't flinch as she calls the next man forward
only to find him asleep on the chair in his curtained-off cubicle.
Shaken awake, Les Noy hands up his card.

She launches into her questions, "Have you ever . . . ?" but
her eyes flick down to the name printed on the card: ROBERT L.
PETTERGREE. She breaks off and looks up at the man, who has
an ordinary, tired sort of face and is swaying a little on his feet.

"Mr. Robert Pettergree? You are Mr. Robert L. Pettergree,
formerly of the Better-Farming Train?"

The man's eyes roll a little from side to side. "That's right,"
he says, not meeting her gaze.

Sister Crock purses her lips for a minute and thinks. It's not
unheard of. There was a circular about impostors from the di-
rector general of recruiting. Unfit men sometimes paid a mate to
do the medical for them so they could get the postwar pension.
But this case isn't about money. From what she knows of Robert
Pettergree he'd be repulsed by the idea of scamming money
from the government. And it isn't about age. She accepted Hec
Bowd, who has a good ten years on Robert Pettergree. Sister
Crock reasons, correctly, that he must have a physical condition
that prevents him from standing before her naked. She goes on
to imagine, incorrectly, an intimate affliction—a botched cir-
cumcision or the like, rather than the more mundane truth of a
pigeon chest. And although she thinks briefly of Jean alone in
some awful farmhouse surrounded by sandy waste (she has been

influenced here by Mr. Ohno's letters—of course she read them all), she respects Robert for his stand and she likes the idea of being in on it. Part of her would like to watch Les Noy's face as she reveals him as a fake, but a bigger part of her is flattered to be part of something so male, so larrikin, so daring.

Sister Crock winks at Les Noy.

"Stand against the measure, please, heels touching." She slides the stick into position. "Funny, isn't it, Mr. Pettergree? You seem to have lost some height in the Mallee."

29

THE MALLEE SUNSET

Some men don't take the seven days to fix up their private affairs. Some go straightaway, hitching a ride on the recruiting train to the next major town and then changing for the city. These are the men Mr. Plattfuss calls publicly "economic recruits," and privately "five-bob-a-day murderers." Their enlistment orders direct them to come in working clothes and bring their own cutlery. Most wear the only clothes they own and are lucky to carry a rusty penknife in their pocket.

Robert wears his good blue suit. His wedding suit. He left without telling me and I wouldn't have known but Sister Crock noticed him waiting around with the other men as they packed up, and she sent Mr. Plattfuss out in the Clectrac with a message. I was so shocked by the news I shut the door in his face. He took off straightaway so as not to miss the train, which meant I had to run across the paddock to Ivers's and get Elsie to drive me to the station. Once I was settled in the front seat and my heart had stopped pounding I knew I wasn't going to plead. There was no point in dragging him back to face the failure.

He'd found some new ideas to deceive himself with and they didn't include me. But I wanted to see him. I wanted to hold him and smell his skin, feel his stubble and the flushed heat of his face against my cheek. I wanted to imprint him on me, to make a last physical memory to draw upon in my grieving.

Elsie drove like an invalid, gripping the wheel as if she were trying to squeeze the life out of it. As we rounded Mount Wycheproof I could already see the engine rolling slowly south, a soft glove of steam trailing behind it.

"Sorry, too late, love," Elsie said, but she kept driving and didn't stop until the car was stalled over the tracks. We watched the train roll farther and farther away from us. Some of the men waved from the windows—one lost his hat to the wind. For a few seconds all our gazes intersected as we watched the hat surf the breeze. It looped and danced and then fell suddenly sideways, landing on its crown in a breath of pink soil.

I didn't see Robert. But he wouldn't have been waving. He wouldn't have been looking out the windows. We watched as the train lost its shape and dipped over the horizon. I wept a little then, but a truck drove up fast behind us with its horn blaring and Elsie had to put her foot down.

We went to the butcher's. Elsie didn't want to waste a trip into town. Then she dropped me home. She patted my shoulder as I reached for the door handle. "I'll send Bill over to help with the heavy things."

"Pardon?"

"For moving. With your husband gone you'll be moving. I'll send Bill over."

Will padded around the side of the house to greet the car.

He'd just woken up and his long snout broke into a toothy yawn.

"I'm not moving, Elsie. He chose to leave, it doesn't mean I have to." I hadn't thought this through at all but speaking it made it clear. I would stay.

Elsie shrugged and brushed an imaginary spot from the sleeve of her dress. "Whatever you say. This is no place for a woman on her own, but whatever you say."

I patted Will, then I ate an orange and slept for a while. When I woke I thought I could hear someone playing the piano—the repeated tinkly jumble, just like Abe walking up and down the keyboard with his three tabby legs and one white leg, but it was only the wind rolling an empty beer bottle backwards and forwards against the step.

Then I went for a walk across the paddocks. I walked in the wheat and remembered what Robert had told me about the break. How each morning close to harvest time the men would walk out into the paddocks, break a wheat stem and listen for a particular sound—a clean dryness—that meant the wheat was ready to harvest. I thought of all the men of the Mallee alone in the early morning listening to the sound of a stem snapping— the sharp, dry sound of it amplified across the paddocks, joining up from farm to farm, coming together distinctly so the towns- folk in their beds would be woken by it. And that everyone would know, instantly, that the pattern of our days was about to change from growing to harvest.

The wheat that is left in our paddocks is poor. There are patches of rust and thin patches where the seed has failed to strike. I am not sure what will happen when it is just left like this, how long it will live, how quickly the other plants will move in to replace it.

I make only two decisions. The first is to ask Ollie Bowd to stay. I can teach her to sew on her old Singer and she can help me with the farm. Perhaps together we can grow a different crop—something that belongs here. And I will go to Tatura and visit Mr. Ohno—fraternize a little with the enemy. I would like to bring him here and show him the farm. Show him that I didn't die in the sandy waste and that perhaps there is something here for me after all.

I take off my shoes and stockings and walk back to the house. The sun is setting but the soil is still warm beneath my feet. In the Mallee there is nothing in between the sun and the soil. It is just like the picture on the boxes of raisins and oranges—strong tentacles of light radiating out in a perfect circle.

The sun sinks lower. A last golden slab of light glances my arm and sweeps warmly down to my feet. Then the air chills quickly. I open the kitchen door and go inside.

ABOUT THE AUTHOR

Carrie Tiffany was born in West Yorkshire, England, and migrated to Western Australia with her family in the early 1970s. She spent her early twenties working as a park ranger in the red center and now lives in Melbourne, where she works as an agricultural journalist.